EVERYTHING IS FINE

(and other lies I tell myself)

Cathy Brett has been scribbling stuff for more than twenty years; as a fashion illustrator, as a jet-setting spotter of global trends and as a consultant to the behemoths of the British high street.

She now lectures in design and unashamedly plunders her students' lives for sensational storylines and characters.

Also by Cathy Brett

Ember Fury
Scarlett Dedd
Verity Fibbs

CATHY BRETT

EVERYTHING
IS
FINE

(and other lies I tell myself)

headline

First published in Great Britain in 2013 by
HEADLINE PUBLISHING GROUP

2

'Anthem for Doomed Youth', 'Futility' and 'Strange Meeting' reproduced
here as they appear in *Wilfred Owen: The War Poems* (Chatto & Windus, 1994),
edited by Jon Stallworthy.

Cataloguing in Publication Data is available from the British Library

ISBN 978 0 7553 7949 1

Typeset in Garamond by Jason Cox

**Printed in Great Britain by
Clays Ltd, St Ives plc**

Headline's policy is to use papers that are natural, renewable and recyclable
products and made from wood grown in sustainable forests. The logging and
manufacturing processes are expected to conform to the environmental
regulations of the country of origin.

HEADLINE PUBLISHING GROUP
An Hachette UK Company
338 Euston Road
London NW1 3BH

www.headline.co.uk
www.hachette.co.uk

For my sister, Nicola

Chapter One

She was close to the edge, too close. A careless gust thrown up from the beach below might catch her, tip her off balance and send her staggering forward or sideways. Her feet might find a loose patch of chalk. She might slip and be carried towards the crumbling rim.

She took a shuddering breath, tipped her head back and groaned.

The spiteful wind snatched her voice away as she forced out

'Uuuuaaahhhh!'

the last dregs of air and purged her lungs.

The pain was still there, a dark, suffocating poison clogging her thoughts and tying knots in her gut. She rubbed the tips of exhausted fingers across her eyelids, pressing hard into the sockets. She swallowed, tasting salt – the salt of the sea and of her tears. The breeze returned to tease her hair and whip it against her neck. A strand found its way into the corner of her mouth. She spat, then scraped it out and tugged it behind her ear. She leaned into the wind and it pushed back stubbornly against her aching limbs. She closed her eyes, sighed and swayed, surrendering.

There was someone behind her. She could feel a shape deflecting the wind and muffling sound. She could sense the heat of their body. She waited for a hand on her shoulder or slipped around the crook of her arm, dragging her to safety. She waited, fearful. Brittle. One touch and she'd lose control again. One touch and she might crumble like the chalk cliff, shatter into tiny pieces and blow away, dust on the breeze. But the touch never came. The figure simply stepped forward and stood beside her, silent, reassuring. Without moving her head she stole a look through trembling hair.

She knew it would be him.

'Don't . . . I can't . . . please . . . I can't . . .' she whispered.

He said nothing.

She sniffed. 'I'm not . . . I wasn't going to, you know . . . if that's what you were thinking. I just . . . just came here to think.'

She stared out across the churning sea.

He said nothing.

'I'm OK,' she said.

But she wasn't OK. She was about as far from OK as it was possible to be. She'd been lying to everyone, lying to herself. She'd been confused, mixed up, and, yes, she'd made mistakes.

All she'd wanted was to make things right again. How had it gone so wrong?

Chapter Two

Four weeks ago

Dear Max,

Last day of school today. Hurrah! Farewell and adieu cell mitosis, French verbs and hideous green blazer.

I finally finished my poetry essay. I was going to title it 'The *Late* Poets of the First World War' but I guess that's a lame joke. You don't get extra grades for lame jokes. Just like I won't get extra grades for having had a week's extension, because I rushed it last night, like I always do, and wrote all this dumb stuff about heroism, realism and rhyming schemes straight out of the study guide. I guess I could have written what I really thought, that poems about wailing shells, drowning in mud, twitching bodies on barbed wire and choking gas are deeply disturbing and SO sick. I could have written that Sassoon made me cry and Edward Thomas made my brain ache and Wilfred Owen broke my heart. Or that Miserable Wilf reminded me of that dude Keats we studied last year and that, in my opinion, Keats wrote the most desperately *emo* poems of all. But I didn't. Well, not in those exact words. So, my essay is a definite C, maybe a D. Who cares? I don't. There are more important things to worry about. Like getting through the summer.

Esther tapped return, then slurped another spoonful of cereal. Milk dripped on her school tie and she brushed it off. Another stain on her uniform was no biggie. In a few hours she'd be discarding it anyway. She stared at the remaining Os floating in the bowl.

Across the kitchen she could hear the shuffle of Mum's flip-flops. She glanced up to see her leaning over the bin, lowering something in.

Mum? Mum's still hopelessly deluded. No change there. She thinks if she keeps her back to me I won't notice that she's trying to hide last night's wine bottles under kitchen waste. But I can hear them clinking against the ones from Tuesday and Monday, and the empties from last weekend.

Plastic wheels rumbled noisily overhead. She looked up, then grimaced at a new sound, the staccato syncopation of a juddering metal pipe gouging plaster.

Dad? Well, Dad's mind has packed its bags and moved to another planet (Neptune, I think). He won't let Mum put this place on the market, but that hasn't stopped his brain moving out. He shambles from room to room, dragging that big industrial vacuum cleaner, and doesn't even notice the brush attachment chipping massive chunks out of the walls.

Most of the time he's kind of a zombie. Yep, we have a zombie dad.

They fight a lot, stupid whispered arguments that go round and round in the same circles, never reaching a conclusion. They think I can't hear them, but I can. Every word. I wish you were home. They'd stop if you were here.

Such is life at the Pebbleton Beach Guest House.

In the very temple of Delight, veiled Melancholy has her sovran shrine.

Is that Miserable Wilf or Emo Keats? I don't remember.

Anyway, something has to change. It will. It must. I've got this feeling, deep down, like an itch or a little voice whispering in my head.

Did little voices whispering in her head make her sound crazy? She scooped up the last of the cereal and regarded the beige puddle that remained. There was always a puddle. It didn't matter how frugal she was with the milk, there would be a lake of the stuff at the bottom when she finished. How might the war poets describe it? she wondered. *A strangling lake of doom, drowning souls. A pool of sludge in the pit of hell, ankle-deep, the pallor of girls' brows.* Maybe she should have written that in her essay.

She smirked, and the clock on the cooker flickered from 8.04 to 8.05. She still had a few minutes. She looked back at the screen, shook her head, pressed 'delete' and held it down.

Last day of school today. Hurrah! Mum's still crazy. Dad is kind of a zombie.

Then wrote:

But I guess you want the Disney version, so they're fine. We're all fine.

7

The door from the empty breakfast room slammed open and a dark-haired boy sock-surfed across the tiled floor, grabbing a bag of bread from the counter as he passed.

'Eeerrrooowww!' he whooped.

Mum stood up straight and the bin rattled.

The boy yanked out two anaemic slices, scattering crumbs, then reached past Esther and slipped them into the toaster. He rammed the handle down, then turned and pushed off again. He skated to the other side of the kitchen, opened a cupboard, extracted a jar of chocolate hazelnut spread and slid something out of his pocket, a glinting object. He gripped one side and unfolded a stubby blade, which clicked into place. Without waiting for the toast, he thrust the knife into the jar and began to lick the spread from the blade. He leered at her then chuckled as he drew the knife slowly across his chocolate-coated tongue.

'Mmmmm.'

Esther turned back to her laptop.

Except Gulliver, who is a dangerous criminal. I mean scary dangerous!

Cold steel . . . thinly drawn with famishing for flesh. Now that *is* Wilf, isn't it?

Better go. Bus. More later.

Love forever etc.

Your mixed-up but devoted sister, Egg x

She closed the laptop and picked up her cereal bowl. Thank goodness she and Gulliver didn't attend the same school any

more, she thought. Although excluding him from one school had just moved the problem up the coast to the Greymouth Academy. She went to the sink, poured the cloying milk down the plughole, then dumped the bowl in the dishwasher.

Kerchunk!

Gulliver's toast leaped up and sprayed more crumbs across the counter. It was bad enough living with a thirteen-year-old psychopath, but imagine sharing the bus, or worse, bumping into him in a corridor or the lunch queue or something.

'Too bad you don't have a nut allergy,' she hissed.

'I do,' said Gulliver, pointing the knife. 'To you, you're the nut.' He clutched the knife in his fist and stabbed at the air.

She sighed and shook her head. 'Freak.'

Mum was no longer preoccupied with the bin. She'd shuffled along the counter and was spooning instant coffee into a mug. It would be pointless telling her about the knife. Gull had been heading for serious trouble for months. At this rate he'd probably be chucked out of another school and have a criminal record before he reached his fourteenth birthday, but Mum couldn't see it. To her he was just a misunderstood, hyperactive kid letting off steam.

Esther leaned down and tugged at her socks, smoothed her hair behind her ears and padded into the laundry corridor, a long, narrow room that ran along the side of the house. It contained two washing machines, a tumble dryer and a chaotic assortment of coats, waterproofs, wellingtons and walking boots hanging on hooks or piled by the back door. She slipped into her school shoes, picked up her bag and reached for the door handle.

'Bye,' she called, but got no reply. She was tired of being ignored and even more tired of treading on eggshells every morning, so she shouted, 'Mum, those wine bottles should go in the recycling.' Then she stepped out into the yard and closed the door behind her, a defiant smile on her face.

Once she'd negotiated the rubbish bins at the side entrance, counted her steps across the car park and got out to the road,

she took her phone from the front pocket of her bag and began to tap out a text to Molly. She'd be sitting next to her friend in a few minutes, when the bus reached the other end of the village, but this was their morning ritual – a greeting, a bit of goss, perhaps a shared viral video or just picking up the thread of the previous night's chat.

Bonjour. End of term!
Yay!

She pressed send, then looked up, shading her eyes with the phone. Something was wrong. The road was empty and silent. The bus was late. She sighed and chewed at her thumbnail. Every morning, as soon as she got outside, she would hear the reassuring grumble of the diesel engine and see the dark green roof sailing above the hedge at the bottom of the hill. She climbed up on to the ridge of the bank beside the road and listened, but there was no engine sound and no green roof. She bit along the nail of her index finger, her teeth making a *pok-pok* sound inside her head.

A tiny black shape flashed through the grass at her feet and she flinched. There, half hidden by a frond, was a black beetle, inky and slick as if dipped in oil. It must have been basking in the morning sunshine when her clumsy footsteps had disturbed it. She watched it as the grass swayed and the frond flapped, but it remained frozen beside her shoe. It could have been one of those insect specimens in a cabinet at the Natural History Museum, a pin skewering it to a board, impaled next to rows of identical oily, shimmering cousins. Suddenly it scuttled away, further along the slope, mercifully un-pierced.

She closed her eyes and inhaled the chalk and sea breeze and warming road tar. It was unusually quiet; the only sound the wind in the grass and the distant sigh of the waves. What would she do if the bus didn't come? What if it had been early and she'd missed it? Her heart fluttered behind her ribs.

She wished for a moment that she could be that beetle, scuttling around in the grass, free to bask in the sun or hide in the shade, not tied to school schedules and bus timetables. Not handing in late poetry essays. The beetle had such a beautiful, tough-looking shell. Having your skeleton on the outside like that must be bliss, she thought. Like wearing armour. Nothing would get through that solid crust to harm the soft flesh inside. Human skin was too thin, too vulnerable.

Why didn't human beings grow shells?

If she'd missed the bus, she decided, she'd cut school and go down to the beach, bask on the dunes, scuttle in the grass, be a beetle for the day. Her heart thumped at the thought of it.

The low rattle of an engine rumbled up the hill.

She let out her breath. Maybe not.

The bus slowed and stopped a few metres short of where Esther was waiting. There was a hiss and the door juddered open.

She jogged along the top of the bank and then leaped down on to the first step, causing the front of the bus to twitch and roll. There was a roar behind her. A sleek black car swung around the corner on the wrong side of the road, head-on to the bus, going much too fast. It was oily black like the darting beetle. The car braked and the driver seemed to lose control, swerving in to clip the bank. The tyres ripping into the soft chalk exactly below the spot where Esther had been standing, churning up the dust. It bounced heavily, then snaked back on to the other side of the road and accelerated away.

She grabbed the handrail and leaped up the remaining steps, then watched through the back window of the bus as the ink-black shape shot down into the village.

'Tourists!' said the bus driver, smiling and shaking his head. 'That was close.'

Esther nodded, then frowned. It wasn't funny. Why was he smiling?

'You all right?' he asked. 'You're white as chalk.'

'Mmm.' She looked down at the bank through the still open door, where the car's tyre had left a scuff mark. There, just visible through the dust, was the black beetle, spinning around in frenzied circles, having missed a gory death under the wheels of the car.

The door juddered shut and she sidled along the aisle looking for a space, manoeuvring past a confusion of knees, feet and bulging school bags. She felt sick. One second you're alive, happy inside your shell and basking in the sun, the next you could be flattened under a car tyre. As she sat down on a scratchy, fabric seat that prickled the back of her knees, her phone buzzed. It was Molly's return text.

Oui. Les grandes vacances. Hurrah! Is bus late? Waiting here 100 years! Mol x

Chapter Three

Every lesson dragged. There was no enthusiasm, not even for the customary games, videos and end-of-term quizzes with chocolate prizes. All minds were distracted, preoccupied with summer plans. Pupils and teachers watched the hands of the classroom clocks clicking lethargically towards the final bell, and when it came, the whole school seemed to exhale, as one. The dam breached, they spilled out to flood the surrounding streets and meander homeward.

The bus was stifling hot, the air heavy and humming with excited but weary chatter. All of the sliding vents at the top of the windows were pushed wide open, but made little impact on the stench of half-eaten sandwiches, banana skins, festering sports kit and armpits. Kids on the sunny side had resorted to finding some shade under coursework folders and rucksacks, while others simply baked in sticky uniforms.

The bus was a cauldron in summer and a swamp in winter, but getting a lift in your parents' car had become desperately unfashionable, so the choice was either take the bus or walk the six miles to the high school. Only the brave and foolish

now cycled, since the road to Stone Harbour had become four lanes of deadly thundering lorries.

Years ago, when Esther had been new to the school, Mum had driven her there, picking up Molly on the way and dropping them both a suitable distance from the gate. But now Mum had to transport Gull to and from Greymouth Academy. She didn't trust Gull to walk there without getting into some mischief or other. Greymouth was in the opposite direction.

Esther tried not to breathe in the fetid air, but arched her neck and lifted her chin, catching the occasional fresher draught and holding it in, as if it might be enough to cool her lungs. She and Molly had removed their ties and shoes, rolled their shirt-sleeves up to their shoulders and peeled off their charcoal knee-socks. Their hated polyester blazers had already been balled up and rammed inside their bags before morning break.

The girls sprawled across the back seat; usually a forbidden territory reserved exclusively by sixth-formers and college students for wrestling – both the fighting and the making-out variety. But the last of the wrestlers had got off two stops before, and Esther and Molly had leaped towards the luxury of shade and leg room. Now they lay across the entire back seat, bare feet touching, their heads propped up on school bags, sucking noisily on the final syrupy ice crystals of super-size SlushBerries. In a blissful sugar haze, they stared out of the windows and watched the landscape sweep by like an anti-tourist advert.

They rumbled past the castle gift shop, where a noisy flock of seagulls pecked at an overflowing waste bin. Then down the hill by the old orchard with the discarded fridge. Then past the blue van, parked on Cove Road, where you could buy fresh crabs during the day and illegal duty-free booze at night. As they turned left at the war memorial, Esther could see the looming white ghost of her own home at the top of the cliff road, the Pebbleton Beach Guest house.

'Look at that. You can see the green slime patch from here,' she moaned.

'Uh?' Molly grunted.

'Where the gutter is broken,' she said. 'That's why nobody wants to stay. Green slime.'

'I think it's *très gentil*,' said Molly. 'Not the green slime, the house.'

'Used to be. Now it's just as shabby as the rest of the village. What a dump.'

'Mmm.'

She couldn't tell if her friend was agreeing or just making a sympathetic noise. 'I mean,' Esther continued, 'you'd stay in one of those shiny places over in Silver Sands, wouldn't you?'

'I suppose so.'

'Somewhere that didn't have worn carpets or peeling paint.'

'Uh-huh.'

Esther paused and thought for a moment. 'I guess nobody would want to buy it in that state either.' She shrugged. 'So maybe it's a good thing . . . the green slime.'

'Mmm.'

'But it kinda looks like the house has a disease or it's cursed or something, doesn't it?'

Molly didn't answer.

They both lapsed into silence.

Esther was annoyed with herself. She said stupid stuff when she was tired. Sometimes she said the first thing that came into her head, however dumb it might be. Molly probably guessed what she really meant, which was that it was the people inside the guest house who were cursed. Well, not cursed exactly. Troubled. Falling apart. Molly understood and would let it go. But one day Esther might say something she didn't mean to say out loud. Like the things she kept to herself, the worries and secret thoughts she couldn't tell anyone, not even Max.

The bus pulled in outside the library and more wilting kids got off. Just a handful remained.

'Es?' said Molly.

'Yeah?'

'If the guest house is practically empty, you're not gonna be working much this summer, are you?'

'I guess not.'

'So you'll have no dosh. I mean, to go *en train à Londres* or something, like we planned?'

She thought for a moment. Molly was right. Last summer the guest house had been full and they'd both earned a bit of extra money working for Dad, serving tea or cleaning bathrooms. They'd made enough for a couple of trips to the shops in Greymouth and to the cinema. They'd even bought new wetsuits.

But that was
last summer.
Last summer
was different.
'What about
your mum?'
Esther asked.
'Does she need
someone else in her shop?'
'I could ask, but it's *un peu
difficile*. I'm already working
two afternoons. She can't
afford more staff unless
we get really busy.

Maybe when she goes to Greymouth for the craft fair.'

'Nah. That's only a weekend. Two days. That's not gonna earn us enough for the train fare to London, is it?'

The brakes hissed and the door flapped shut.

Esther slumped down further on the seat until she was almost lying flat. She didn't really want a job. She'd rather curl up in the sand dunes all summer and do nothing. Maybe read a book or two, surf when the waves were right and work out how to put her family back together again.

'Wait!' Molly shouted at the driver. 'Open the door. We're getting off.' She turned to her friend. 'Come on.'

'Wha'?' Esther raised her head and opened her eyes.

'We're getting off here,' said Molly.

'Urrgh. Too hot,' Esther complained, shading her face from the mid-afternoon glare. 'Can't climb the hill in this heat.'

'We have to check the newsagent's window for summer jobs.'

Esther sighed. Molly seemed to have endless supplies of energy. And she was annoyingly enthusiastic about everything.

'We can get ice cream,' said Molly. 'Ice cream always cheers you up.'

'OK.' She rolled off the seat and picked up her bag. 'Pistachio. Two scoops, and it's your turn to pay.'

There were lots of cards and flyers in the newsagent's window, but few of them were ads for summer jobs.

FOR SALE

Children's inflatable paddling pool, toys and games, good condition

Call Laura 0   36129974

J C Blezzard

Friendly Local Plumber

Competitive rates No job too small

03   9969   49576

         Road Pebbleton

GREEN FINGERS
GARDEN MAINTENANCE

LADYBIRDS PLAYGROUP

CHURCH HALL weekday mornings

CRB checked helpers needed
CALL Sally 02756 3439356

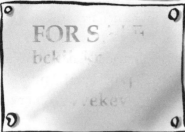

FOR SALE

FRESH CRABS

PICTURES *of* **PEBBLETON**
Photographic Exhibition

Village Life through the Ages

Pebbleton Museum
1st July - 31st August

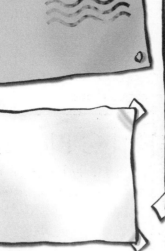

25

The best jobs – shop assistant at the Big Wave Surf Store or selling tickets for Smuggler's Rock Boat Tours – stated 'experience essential'. There would be no point even applying for them, because they always went to uni students. A restaurant in Silver Sands was looking for waitresses, but you had to be over eighteen for that too. Even wearing heels, lipstick and a padded bra, Esther knew she'd never pass for eighteen.

'I hate being short,' she said.

'You're not short, you're petite,' said Molly, dipping her plastic spoon into their shared tub of green mush.

Esther snorted. 'Huh. That's what my mum says. But it

doesn't matter what you call it. Being *petite* is rubbish. My legs are spaghetti and my . . .' She looked enviously at her curvy friend. 'Well, I've got mozzie bites instead of . . .'

Molly folded her arms over her chest and hunched her shoulders. 'Yeah? You wanna try being Molly Funbags for a while? It's *pas amusant*.' She rolled her eyes.

They made a last futile scan of the patchwork of cards behind the glass.

'Nope. Nothing.' Esther waved her spoon lethargically. She hadn't inserted it into the ice cream yet and probably wouldn't. The boy who'd served them in the shop wasn't the same one who'd been there last time. It wasn't the ice cream that had cheered Esther up before, it had been the boy that worked there. He'd been delicious, with smooth, sun-bronzed skin and grey eyes like ice chips. Much tastier than the sickly, artificially coloured desserts he sold. Now he'd gone – probably got a place at some university the other side of the country – and the new boy, Esther noticed, had black-edged fingernails. Eergh! She'd let Molly eat it all.

'Beach?' she suggested, feeling defeated.

'Oh yeah, great idea! *Sur la plage, sur le Wipeout!*' said Molly, jabbing her spoon towards Esther's head.

'What? The Wipeout Café? You still hungry, then?' Esther frowned.

'No, dummy, you could get a job there. I heard Finch is looking for an assistant.'

'OK.' Esther tugged her shirt and flapped air under the hem until it inflated around her inadequate chest. 'But we've got to get out of these uniforms first.'

Chapter Four

She kicked off her shoes and flung them behind the back door, then lassoed her bag strap over the hook above. She had detoured around the back of the house then sneaked in through her secret side entrance. It had originally been Max's secret side entrance – a narrow gap between two outbuildings – but now it was hers. It was dark, dirty and lined with cobwebs, so she'd emerged into the yard even hotter and dustier. She couldn't wait to discard her uniform and take a shower.

The house was weirdly silent, just its old bones and the roof tiles cracking in the heat and the *click click click* of the washing machine as the drum turned over and something – probably a button – repeatedly hit the glass door. As she slouched across the lobby and headed for the stairs, she noticed the low hum of voices coming from the lounge. She moved closer, intrigued.

Was it Mum with some of her waste-of-space friends helping her to drink this weekend's case of Chardonnay? Or were they new guests? There was a male voice, but it wasn't Dad's. He'd probably escaped to his boathouse for an hour or two to smoke a furtive cigarette and work on his model boats.

She stood behind the door and peered into the lounge through the crack by the doorframe. Perhaps it was an executive on a business trip to Greymouth looking for somewhere a little cheaper to stay. They got people like that from time to time. No. Mum was talking to a man and a woman. They weren't her boozy mates either, but they didn't look like the usual B&B guests. This couple were too well dressed for weekend sailors or hikers. They should have been staying at a glitzy place in Stone Harbour or renting a big house on the coast road. Maybe they were a cheating couple in search of a secret weekend hideaway. If so, why were they chatting with Mum in the lounge?

Esther felt a little shiver of excitement. At last something interesting might have walked through the guest house door. Perhaps her summer wouldn't be six weeks of terminal boredom after all.

The man was talking on a mobile phone and had casually flipped a pair of expensive sunglasses on to the top of his head so that his gelled hair stuck out like a lion's mane. No sensible cliff walker or cyclist would wear such flimsy shades. They'd be grabbed by the sea breeze and flung over the nearest cliff. And anyone that pretentious looking would be laughed right out of the Castle Bike Shop. The woman had lots of clinking wooden bangles around her wrists and kept scraping her fingers through glossy butter-blond hair.

Outsiders. Definitely.

Esther's excitement was growing.

'Yeah, parking is fine,' said the man into his phone. 'We may have to widen the entrance a bit and dig up a couple of hedges … Uh-huh, no problem-o …' He snapped the phone shut.

'So we'll be in touch,' said the woman.

'OK,' said Mum. She shook hands with both of the strangers and they began to walk towards the door.

Esther ran across to the stairs and sprinted up to the first landing,where she hid behind the banister rails. She could hear the faint sound of Gulliver on the top floor, playing some war game on his computer.

'Die! Die!' he yelped.

Mum followed the couple across the lobby to the front door, and Esther edged over to the landing window. That was when she saw the car, a black Mercedes, in the car park. It was the one that she'd seen that morning, the one that had almost wrecked the bus and squashed the beetle. She swallowed then ran up the stairs to her room, her heart beating like crazy.

Everything happens for a reason, she thought. She'd been waiting for a sign, something to confirm what she'd suspected, the strange feeling she'd had for weeks. Something important was going to happen this summer, something that would solve all their problems. Now here was the sign, in their car park, the black car.

She pushed through the door marked 'PRIVATE' and ran up the last flight of steps. The family lived in six tiny rooms at the front and top of the building. Her bedroom window had a great view of the drive. If the Mercedes couple were checking in, she'd watch them get their luggage, see if it gave her any clues, then sneak back down, when they were in their rooms, to find out more about them. Why were they here? Were they from London? Perhaps they had their own company – something glamorous like fashion or shoes – and were looking for an assistant, and they wouldn't mind that she was only fifteen. She'd drop out of school and go back to London with them and start a new, exciting life in the city.

She went to her window and pressed her nose against it, fogging the glass with her breath.

Maybe they worked for a big publishing house and she could give them that stack of notebooks with the stories she'd been writing and they'd love them and want to publish them and she'd leave school and be an author and have her own luxurious writing hut on the beach.

A rattle of gunfire leaked through the wall from Gull's room. The couple below crunched across the gravel and the black beetle blinked and beeped. They gripped handles, opened the doors wide. There was a muffled landmine explosion next door as Esther's excitement evaporated. They weren't getting luggage, they were getting into the car, closing the doors, starting the engine, pulling away and leaving. They weren't guests. They must have changed their minds, she thought. And who could blame them?

The expensive car turned right and headed towards the ferry, and she slumped down on her bed, deflating like a punctured balloon. She sighed and leaned back. Her knuckle grazed the cold edge of her laptop. Mum had brought it up from the kitchen. She opened it and pressed the power button. Then she plugged in her headphones to drown out the extreme violence being perpetrated in Gulliver's room.

Dear Max,

Miserable and bored. This summer is going to be awful.

Gull is committing mass murder next door. No surprise there. He's a freak. How will I ever avoid him for the whole holiday? I just know he's going to irritate me to death. I may just explode. I can't imagine how you shared a tent with him at the Smuggler's Rock Festival last year without going insane. I'm pretty certain I would have strangled him. Or worse.

I'm listening to your summer playlist while I write, and it's rubbish. The Smiths? Really? But you know me. I'll listen to anything that doesn't make my ears bleed!!! Ha ha!

There was a bit of excitement here just now. I thought we might get some proper guests. They had this posh car and everything, not the usual muddy mountain bikes. But, of course, it turns out they decided not to stay.

Esther winced and felt a shiver of fear.

Unless they were estate agents. Oh no! I think Mum might have put the house on the market without telling us. Without telling Dad! How could she? It's SO typical. Now I'm miserable, bored and totally furious with Mum.

You would have liked their car, though, a black Mercedes.

Gotta go. Meeting Mol at Wipeout.

Love etc.

The Egg-ster x

Chapter Five

Wipeout was buzzing. The café beside the dunes car park had once been a derelict beach hut, then, briefly, a soft drinks kiosk. Later, its new owner, Finch, had added several quirky extensions to the building, transforming it into a funky beach café. He'd built a rickety veranda at the front and installed half a caravan at the back, to serve as the kitchen. He had nailed reclaimed window frames together to form a sort of low-rent conservatory on the side and wedged brightly painted scaffolding poles under the hotchpotch of corrugated-iron that formed the roof.

Finch was not just a café owner. He was a musician, an artist and an eccentric. His vivid abstract paintings filled the walls inside the shack, and scattered all around the building was his 'collection' – accumulated flotsam and jetsam, weird and wonderful items found washed up on the beach: painfully knotted driftwood, lost

oars, pitted plastic buoys, torn fishing nets, sun-bleached floats, plastic crabs, doll's heads, inflatable sharks, rubber pineapples, water pistols, castle-shaped buckets and orphan flippers. When inspiration struck, he'd fasten items together with wire to create an extraordinary multi-limbed sculpture, which he'd sell for hundreds of pounds to a Silver Sands gallery.

Considering the proprietor was a musician, Wipeout's sound system was extremely primitive. Finch had found a discarded ancient radio/CD player on the beach and had hung it from the rafters of the veranda. The CD slot was jammed with sand but he'd painted it with a multicolour zigzag pattern and tuned the radio to Stoneharbour FM, a hip-hop station. The sounds it emitted ensured that the café was given a wide berth by pensioners and young families, but guaranteed the patronage of Pebbleton's teens.

Near the veranda, slick, wetsuit-clad youths basked on plastic chairs in the late afternoon sun, like a family of seals. They were flirting clumsily with three tanned girls; brightly coloured, twittering birds of paradise. The girls were obviously Outsiders who'd taken the ferry over from Silver Sands. Locals would never wear such lurid bikinis or tease their dyed white-blond hair into dishevelled side plaits. Nor did Esther and Molly's friends frequent the Silver Sands spray-tan booths, where pale bodies could be sprayed once, twice, maybe more, until they resembled preserved orange peel.

'Huh. Outsiders,' huffed Molly.

'Mmm,' Esther agreed, and scowled.

The seals and birds sat at two adjacent plastic tables. Molly and Esther approached the third as a skinny boy got reluctantly to his feet under the awning. He was the only boy in the group not in a wetsuit, the black sling cradling his left arm suggesting a reason. The chatter stopped and they all watched as, one-handed, he raised his T-shirt and eased down the waistband of his jeans to reveal a huge purple bruise from armpit to hip.

'Woah! Cheesy!' someone exclaimed.

'Nice colour!' said another, enviously.

The orange-skinned girls gasped and the injured boy flashed an embarrassed smile and yanked down the shirt. He sat down.

The boy was a new face. Esther recognised all the others, his friends, who went to the college in Pinechester where Max had done his A levels. They whistled and cheered, urging the bruised boy to tell the girls his story. But he looked down at his feet, uncomfortable in the glare of so much attention.

'I saw that wave coming,' said one friend.

'Yeah, it was massive, wasnit?' said another.

'Cheesy!'

'Too scary for me, man, but I thought you'd make it, for sure.'

'So did I,' said the boy, attempting a smile and lifting his damaged arm.

'You really went for it.'

'Yeah. Well next time I'm gonna nail it.'

'Oh wow! Did you nearly drown?' Molly gasped, her eyes wide and her hands held to her face in horror.

There she goes, thought Esther. Molly had launched into her usual flirting routine. She tilted her head, blinked and smiled. She was fearless. She didn't blush and stammer and act like a total idiot in front of boys, like a normal person. It was infuriating. No hesitation, just *voom*, straight in with the smile and the head tilt. She found it so easy to chat to boys, even older boys that she'd never met before, boys who were tall and shy and skinny with damaged arms and bruised ribs, boys who were really cute.

'My board knocked me out,' said the cute bruised boy, and returned her smile.

Esther blew out her cheeks, exasperated. She raised her hand and began to chew the corner of her thumbnail.

The boy touched the side of his head. 'And I was unconscious for 'bout a minute, they reckon.'

'You were under for longer than that,' said another boy. 'More like five.'

'Couldn't have been *five*,' jeered another.

'Yeah, five minutes underwater and you'd be *complètement dead. Mort* as a doornail,' said Molly. She giggled, and Esther pursed her lips.

'Paramedic said I might have died,' said the boy. There were more gasps of awe from the orange-peel-tan girls, but Esther

39

noticed a change in the boy's expression. There
was a tension in his jaw, a small frown line
between his brows. He reminded her
of Max. She looked across the dunes
towards the sea and the foaming
waves, and imagined the boy
under the water, thrown
against rocks, his lungs
bursting. A cold
fist clenched
her stomach.

'Finch says he's sorry but they don't need anyone,' said Molly.

'What?' Esther jumped. How long had she been staring into the distant dazzling water, shimmering across the bay like a sequined dress laid out on a bed? A few seconds, a minute? She blinked and refocused on retreating black silhouettes – the injured boy and his mates walking away down to the beach, carrying their surfboards.

Her throat ached and her eyes were stinging. It might have been longer.

She looked up and squinted.

'He's already hired a new assistant.' Molly was holding two Magnums in front of her and waggling them from side to side. 'Nut or caramel?' she asked. 'I'll have the nut if you want the caramel.'

'I think I might have a cheeseburger instead,' said Esther, patting her belly. She didn't really want a burger but perhaps, she thought, the clench in her stomach was hunger. 'I'll start levitating if I eat any more frozen carbs,' she chuckled.

'Aw!' Molly whined. 'You didn't say anything about a cheeseburger. Now I don't want these either.' She sneered at the choc ices.

'You're a veggie, you twit!'

Molly pouted. 'I know, but I like the melted *fromage*. And the bun.'

Esther snorted and grabbed the caramel Magnum. 'You're priceless, Mol!'

They were still at Wipeout as the sun dipped behind the cliff. Plunged into cool blue shadow, the girls shivered, stroked goose-flesh arms and considered an immediate move down the beach to catch the last warmth of the day. The surfers would soon be heading for shore and the dunes would fill with friendly banter, larking, teasing, jousting, snogging. The holiday had begun.

Esther leaned forward to stand up and something fluttered in her lap. Not fluttered, buzzed. Another beetle? Her shoulders tensed. There it was again, a buzzing against her belly. It was her phone. She pulled it from her pocket, looked at the screen and groaned.

'Your mum checking up on you again?' Molly asked.

'No. I mean, yeah. It's Mum. She wants me to come home.'

Molly leaned over, grabbed her friend's hand and peered down at the screen. 'Family dinner and exciting news,' she read. 'What does that mean?'

'I dunno.'

Esther was ready to text back that she'd already eaten, but the 'exciting news' bit was hard to ignore. That was obviously why Mum had written it. She often tried to get the family to eat together but rarely pulled it off. Family meals were torture and Mum knew that Esther couldn't even be lured home with take away favourites any more – pizza or a bucket of fried chicken.

She began to wonder what Mum would consider 'exciting news'. Gull had got a decent set of grades in his school report – like *that* would ever happen. Mum was going into rehab – just as unlikely. Mum was pregnant. Oh God, she hoped that wasn't it!

'Perhaps a coachload of old biddies has checked in,' Molly suggested.

'That's not exciting news, it's hideous.' She frowned and stood up.

'A coachload of lottery winners,' said Molly, also getting to her feet.

'Nah.' She looked up at the far cliff. The roof of the guest house was just visible above the trees.

'Lottery winners in limousines.'

'Limousines?' Esther shuddered. Molly had jogged her memory. She'd forgotten all about the couple in the inky-black Mercedes. As soon as she'd left the house she'd sort of wiped them from her mind. They'd gone, so that was that.

'The beetle,' she mumbled.

'What?'

'Um, nothing. Just something earlier that I forgot to tell you.'

'About beetles?'

'No, about a car and people from London.'

'London? How could you forget to tell me about people from London?'

'Well, because they've gone. I mean, they drove off . . . back to London. And they might not even be from London. I think Mum might be selling the guest house. They could have been, you know, buyers . . . or estate agents.'

'Estate agents?'

'Dunno. And stop repeating everything.' She pushed Molly away. 'You sound retarded.'

Molly staggered backwards, then turned and started towards a path that led back up to the car park.

'Sorry,' Esther shouted after her. Had she pushed too hard? Had she said something unkind or thoughtless? She was doing that a

46

lot lately. Mum's message had made her feel uneasy, on edge, a bit snappy. 'I didn't mean to push you. Don't get all moody.'

'I'm not moody, I'm interested. Aren't you? Come on,' said Molly, and kept walking.

Esther wasn't interested, she was apprehensive. Did she want to hear Mum's news? News was never good. She'd rather stay on the beach and pretend she hadn't got the text, but Molly was already crossing the dunes car park.

'Where you going?'

'*A votre maison* to find out, dummy.'

'Find out? Find out what?'

'Duh! Now *you* sound retarded.' Molly looked back and smiled. 'To find out what "exciting news" means.'

Chapter Six

Esther and Molly walked into the kitchen as Mum was going out the opposite door.

'Ah, there you are,' said Mum, over her shoulder. 'Hello, Molly, you staying for dinner?'

'Yeah. I mean, yes please, if there's enough for me. Thanks.'

'There's plenty. It's lasagne . . . meat lasagne. But I suppose you can have salad and bread, can't you? Why don't you check with your mum, then you and Esther can bring an extra plate. Oh, and the garlic bread that's in the oven. We're on the terrace.'

The door to the breakfast room swung shut and Mum's voice trailed off into the garden.

'OK,' Molly called.

They looked at each other.

'She seems unusually happy,' said Molly brightly.

'And sober,' said Esther. 'Did she have make-up on?'

'Uh-huh.'

'And she wasn't wearing pyjama bottoms.'

'Nope. Jeans.'

'So what's going on? Something weird has happened.'

'Uh-huh.' Molly nodded.

'She said we're eating on the terrace, right?'

'Yup.'

'So you lose. We only eat on the terrace when the house is empty, so your theory about a coach load of guests is wrong.'

'Yeah.' Molly shrugged.

'And garlic bread. She hasn't made lasagne and garlic bread since . . . well, for months.'

'Let's go and find out.'

Outside, the long table on the terrace was set more for a celebration than a family meal. There were polka dot napkins folded across each plate, a posy of roses and daisies arranged in a jug and even candles flickering in glass jars. Mum positioned the enormous dish of lasagne in the centre of the table with a flourish, as if she was acting in a play. The terrace was her stage and Mum was the star. Esther braced herself for her performance.

Next to the pan of rapidly cooling lasagne was a bowl of salad, from which Gulliver had already extracted all of the red peppers. He had a smug look on his face, which Esther suspected was more than just satisfaction at his conquest of the salad bowl. He already knew what this was about. How annoying. Her disgusting brother was somehow in on Mum's secret. She sat down and scowled at him.

'Dulliver.'

'Fester,' he replied.

'Original,' Esther sneered.

He switched his attention to Molly as she sat down. 'Funbags.'

'Ape,' said Molly with a nod and a smirk.

Hey!' said Esther, noticing what her brother was wearing. 'That's not yours.' She pointed at Gull's sweatshirt.

'So?' He pulled at the neckline. 'It's not yours either, and I like it.'

The sweatshirt was pale blue, well worn, with a swirling orange logo on the front that had faded to sickly beige. It was just readable: SMUGGLER'S ROCK FESTIVAL 2011.

'Liking it doesn't give you permission to wear it,' she spat. 'And stop yanking it like that. You'll pull it out of shape.'

Gull looked skywards and shrugged. 'It's already out of shape. That's why I like it.' He closed his mouth into a smug, straight-line grin.

Esther folded her arms and raised a thumb from the crook of her elbow. She pointed it accusingly at her brother. 'This is why we don't eat together,' she explained to Mum. 'Because *that* puts me off my food.'

'Leave him alone,' said Mum. 'It's only a sweatshirt.'

'But it's Max's sweatshirt.'

Gull pulled at the neckline again and Mum frowned. 'Esther's right, Gull. Don't stretch it like that.' Then she blinked, wriggled her shoulders and surveyed the table in front of her. She'd been diverted from her prepared script.

51

Esther sighed and fed Mum the line she knew she wanted. 'So what's your exciting news?'

'Not yet,' said Mum. 'Wait for Dad.'

Right on cue, Dad slouched into the garden, clutching a plastic folder. He was hunched and gaunt, a desiccated husk, like someone had stuck a SlushBerry straw into his skull and sucked all his juice out.

Mum beamed at him. 'Michael. You won't need to worry about those accounts any more,' she announced.

She never called Dad Michael. Not unless there were important people in earshot. People that Mum thought were important, like headmasters or local politicians. But there was only Molly. She didn't need to impress Molly. Something was up.

'Mmm?' Dad sat and stared at his plate with hollow eyes.

Instead of sulking in the privacy of the boathouse, it seemed that Dad had been in the office stressing over the guest house accounts again. He stabbed feebly at the salad until he'd speared a stack of pale green leaves on his fork. Mum took a deep breath.

'We had visitors today,' she said, a smile twitching across her lips. 'They had an exciting proposition.'

Esther sat up. Mum was talking about the couple in the car. 'You mean those people in the black Mercedes?' she asked.

Mum nodded.

'Not estate agents?' Dad looked concerned. 'I'm not selling, Tess.' He pushed the lettuce off the prongs on to his plate.

'No. Don't worry.'

Esther frowned. She'd guessed wrong. So who were they?

Dad's shoulders dropped. 'Did they check in?' he asked.

'No.'

'Well, what then?' Dad was losing patience.

'Better than that,' said Mum. 'Scouts.'

'What?'

'Location scouts. They were from London, from a film company.'

'See!' Esther gasped. She turned to Molly. 'I *told* you they were from London, didn't I?'

'Did they get lost?' said Dad.

'No.'

'Their sat nav send them up the wrong road?' Dad sniggered.

'Look, just listen, will you,' Mum snapped. 'Do you remember, when we moved here, I signed up with that film location thingy online? You know, the people that find houses for movies?'

Esther's stomach did a somersault.

'You're not saying someone wants to film *here,* are you?' said Dad.

'Actually, they do!'

'Wow!' Molly exclaimed. 'That's . . . that's *très* awesome! You used to be an actress, didn't you, Mrs Armstrong.'

'Tess,' Mum cooed. 'Call me Tess, Molly darling.'

'She only went to drama college for a year,' said Esther.

'The Royal Academy of Dramatic Art, thank you,' said Mum, sliding her hands around her neck then flicking her hair out behind her.

'Then she met Dad and got pregnant with Max, so she didn't do much real acting.'

'I did some telly,' Mum asserted.

'She means she walked across the square in EastEnders.' Esther rolled her eyes.

Mum picked up the bottle of white wine and splashed some into her glass. 'Let's get back to our visitors, shall we?' She took a large mouthful, swallowed and glared at her daughter, clearly annoyed that they'd veered off course again. She put the glass down and continued. 'They were going to film somewhere else, further up the coast, but it all went pear-shaped so they needed a new location kind of urgently. They'd already decided to use Stone Harbour and Pebbleton village for some outside shots, so they were trying to find a suitable house nearby. They chose ours.' She threw her arms out wide and looked up proudly at the building.

'But it's not a house,' said Dad, frowning. 'It's a guest house.'

'Well, right now it's an empty guest house,' said Mum. 'If

you don't want their money, Mike, why don't you call and tell them. Here.' She slapped a thick business card down on the table, then folded her arms and glared at him.

'How much?' Dad asked.

'Enough,' said Mum.

'Enough for what?'

'Enough for you to stop stressing about it being empty all summer. They're going to fix the place up and they'll redecorate when they leave. They'll put it back to exactly the way it was.' Mum's eyes sparkled. 'Or better.'

'Put it back?' Dad was unconvinced. 'That means they are going to change things.' He gripped the sides of his plate with both hands, his white knuckles pushed against his sun-dried skin.

'Not everywhere. Just the front entrance, the lobby and the lounge to begin with, I think.'

Dad nodded and ground his teeth together like a cow chewing grass.

'I might persuade them to film in the garden so they have to repaint the outside as well,' said Mum.

Esther's heart was drumming against her T-shirt, like it was trying to get out. This is it, she thought. This was the thing she knew was coming. Mum was right. This film company might be the answer to all their problems. Dad would stop worrying about money, Mum might stop drinking so much, and she would have a summer job looking after the movie people.

'We'll have to hire back some of the staff we let go at Easter,' Mum continued.

'I can help,' said Esther. 'Like last year.'

Mum raised her eyebrows. 'OK, if you want to. Kitchen or rooms?'

'Kitchen.' She noticed Gulliver was still looking smug. 'You knew all about this, didn't you?'

'Uh-huh.'

'Actually, they want Gull to be in the movie as an extra,' said Mum proudly. She reached out and put her arm around his shoulder.

'Yep,' said Gulliver, shrugging her off and stuffing a forkful of pasta into his mouth. 'I have exactly the right look, apparently.'

'You mean they were looking for apes?' Esther made a disgusted face. 'It's a monkey movie?' She laughed, trying not to give away that she was fuming with jealousy. Why hadn't *she* been there when the film people had arrived? Why hadn't she gone into the lounge instead of hiding on the stairs like a coward? Maybe they would have asked *her* to be in the movie instead of her idiot brother. Surely that was what should have happened.

'Who's in it?' asked Molly. 'Who are the actors? Is there someone famous?'

'What's the film about?' asked Esther.

'I don't know. They didn't say,' said Mum. 'We'll find out soon enough. They move in at the end of next week.'

Dear Max,

Good news first or bad news?

Here's the good. You're not going to believe it. A movie is going to be made in our house! OUR HOUSE! A real film with famous actors in it, that'll be shown in cinemas and everything.

The bad news is that they've asked Gulliver to play a part. He's actually going to act. I know, horrendous, right? Mum was all over him at dinner just now, all proud and smiley and nauseating. Just like when you got your place at uni, remember?

Anyway, we'll get to meet some actual movie stars and it will probably make me the most popular girl in the village and everyone will want to know me because I'll be friends with famous actors and then I expect we'll be invited to the movie premiere in London and have to walk up the red carpet. And we'll watch the film and say 'that is our house, we live there'. How cool is that?!

Eek! I've just become one of those screaming celeb-worshipping fan girls we both hate so much! That's it, Max! It's all over! There's no hope for me now! LOL.

Love etc.

Egg x

Chapter Seven

Esther and Molly linked arms and strode down the path, falling into step as if marching into battle. It was a battle, of sorts. They were marching to join their friends gathering on the shoreline for the start of the summer holiday beach campaign.

It was the same every year. The beach was theirs through the long winter. The local kids owned it, populated it through rain, gales, sleet and ice storms. The windswept beach and the wild dunes were their sole domain until spring. Then the invasion would start. Easter weekend sometimes, if the weather was good. Day-trippers from the city and weekend sailors came first, then holidaymakers staying for a week or more. As the days grew longer and warmer, the Outsiders would pepper the sand with their plastic cool-boxes and tartan blankets. They'd arrange garden chairs, folding tables and beach umbrellas on a carpet of towels, like a seaside version of their own homes. The shallow waves closest to the beach would begin to crawl with clumsy novice surfers, paddling, wobbling, tumbling and splashing. Between them bizarre inflatables would bob and drift, regularly carrying goose-pimpled swimmers out into dangerous currents.

That was when the campaign would begin. In this battle the artillery was youthful exuberance and the military strategy was mild intimidation with a small amount of biding their time, because at the end of each day the kids and the parents would pack up their inflatables and their cool-boxes and head for their cars, and the locals could once again claim back the mile-long beach and maze of dunes. Pebbleton Beach belonged to them, it was their sovereign territory, and they would defend it with all means at their disposal.

When Esther and Molly arrived, the operation had already begun. It was a perfect evening, balmy and golden, and the Outsiders seemed reluctant to leave. The locals were doing their best to encourage their departure. They waded in noisy flocks at the water's edge or perched on surfboard barricades in the dunes, laughing, trying to look intimidating and launching the occasional volley of careless vulgarity across the beach.

The sand dunes were the supply trenches. Some of the boys had carried bricks, metal grilles and sacks of charcoal down the path and had begun to build fire pits. Others had dragged chairs and bits of old carpet to furnish their dugouts. There was even a faded sofa, though its upholstery was worn through to the frame and it looked too uncomfortable to sit on. Their final weapon was music. A rhythmic *kshh kshh kshh kshh* crashed out across the sand and the tourists, at last, began their retreat.

'Hey, Funbags,' called one of the older boys stalking by the water.

His bird-legged friends sniggered. Molly stuck out her tongue and turned, with her nose in the air in mock outrage, pulling her friend in the other direction.

She ran up the beach and began to climb a steep sandbank. Esther guessed where she was going, their favourite spot, and trotted after her. Molly scrambled to the top on her knees then pulled her friend up behind her. Though

Esther dug in her toes, her feet slipped and sent an avalanche of sand down the bank. Finally they both stood up on the rough grass, the wind whipping at their hair and their feet right on the edge. They were now three or four metres above the beach, the expanse of sand stretched out below. From here they could watch the entire scene, feeling a little like mustachioed generals surveying the battlefield.

They sat down and dangled their feet over the cliff, then watched in silence as the last tourist drifted away with the receding tide and the campaign to reclaim the beach stood down. The older boys who'd been hovering at the water's edge slipped off, carrying six-packs of beer, to their dens among the dunes, while others wandered back towards the Wipeout

Café for Finch's famous barbecue-baked potatoes. Esther spotted the college friends in their wetsuits further along the shoreline, the bruised boy with his dark sling easy to identify among them. They were heading towards the dunes too. Some younger kids sent fielders out on to the expanding sand flats and a late afternoon cricket match began – Cove Road versus Castle Estate. They'd probably get in several innings before the tide turned back again.

Esther gazed out to the thin lace edge of the waves in the

distance, and watched it breathing in and out. She matched it with her own breath. In and out, she counted each pulse. In. Out. In. Out.

A pulse in the eternal mind.

Which of the war poets wrote that? she wondered. She couldn't remember.

And each slow dusk a drawing down of blinds.

She shook her head. No more sad poetry. No more war. She was finished with that gloomy essay. It was written, delivered, forgotten. She didn't have to think about school at all until the autumn. No more hiding in the toilets until the break-time bell. No more flicking rubbers in art just so she'd be sent out to stand in the hallway until she decided to 'behave like a grown-up'. What was so good about behaving like a grown-up anyway? Grown-ups were liars. They'd say one thing when they meant something else. They'd pretend to be happy when inside they were all dried up and twisted like Finch's driftwood.

A gust of wind picked up her hair and flipped it across her face, so she scraped it back and hooked it behind her ear. She leaned backwards and the rough grass crackled against her jeans. Putting her hands down to her sides, she ran them across the rasping blades. She felt the tiny teeth along each leaf as it scratched at the skin on her palms, relishing how it tickled at first then bit deeper into her flesh. She plunged her fingers into the soft, yielding sand. It was clean and warm on the surface, but the further down she pushed, the colder it became, cold and damp and putrid.

She shivered and wrenched her hands out. She glanced at Molly, then looked back at the sea. Now. She had to ask now.

She couldn't hold it in any longer.

'Mol, what was it like when your parents split?' She stared at the waves. It wasn't the first time she'd discussed divorce with her friend, but they tended to skirt around the subject, diverting to the circumstances of other school friends rather than their own lives.

Molly swung her legs. 'OK. I don't remember much. Dad left when I was six. One day he was there and the next he wasn't.'

'Oh.'

'I had nightmares for while. I remember that.'

'Yeah?'

'Uh-huh.' Molly raised her knees and clasped her arms around her shins. She rested her chin and it forced her bottom lip out into a pout.

'Did you . . .' Esther shifted nervously on the grass. She knew she was making Molly uncomfortable, but she had more questions. 'Did you, like, want them to stay together?'

'I guess so, at first. But Mum was happier when he left, so . . . They get on all right now.'

'And you see your dad?'

'Not so much since he moved to Newcastle. But we text and talk on the phone all the time, and we meet for birthdays and Christmas and all that.'

Esther wasn't reassured. Was having divorced parents a good or a bad thing? It would be good if it made them happier, but a disaster if it meant they couldn't stay in their home.

Mum and Dad had always run the guest house together, as a team, a partnership. But these days it was like they were living separate lives. They hardly spoke to each other, and when they did, they disagreed. If they split up – as Esther was pretty certain they would – they'd have to sell the house.

Moving from Pebbleton was . . . unthinkable.

So, she wouldn't think about it. She wouldn't think about divorce either. She shook her head.

'You excited about the movie?' she asked.

'Yeah.' Molly released her legs, leaned back and smiled. 'Dad thinks it's so cool!'

Esther laughed. 'That's because it *is* cool. It's the coolest thing EVER!'

Chapter Eight

Dear Max,

It's today! They start shooting today!

At last all that drilling and sawing has stopped in the lounge. I researched online about the story – or the screenplay, as we movie people call it. If you thought it was going to be some Hollywood blockbuster then you'll be disappointed. Apparently it's a 'period drama', set a hundred years ago, so I assumed there would be lots of gorgeous costumes and all that, like long dresses and stuff. But Mum says most of the characters are boys and will be wearing army uniforms because it's all about the First World War. I expect it'll be seriously gloomy, a dullsville month-long history lesson. Yawn.

Did I mention that some of the crew are staying here, in the house? So I've got a summer job after all. Not the actors, of course. They're at one of those swanky places in Stone Harbour. At least Mum and Dad are occupied again and they don't fight so much now we have guests. I still wish you were home, though.

I hear cars.

She closed her laptop and went to the window.

It was early, a little after five thirty in the morning, but a crowd had gathered by the gate for the first day of shooting. News that the actors were finally making an appearance had quickly spread through Pebbleton village, and almost every resident seemed to have risen at dawn to catch a glimpse of the arriving celebrities.

She had always thought their car park was enormous, but today it seemed really tiny, like it was part of the model village in Pinechester. It was packed tight with lorries, vans, caravans and bits of lighting equipment, and the crew scurried back and forth like bees on honeycomb.

She had already helped Dad to feed them all with twenty pots of tea, a gallon of coffee and hundreds of slices of toast, though they'd been warned that the crew would probably want breakfast all over again in a few hours. Film crews were always hungry. Now they, and the yawning star-spotters, were waiting, watching the road for approaching vehicles.

She scanned the crowd from her window. A soft morning mist had almost cleared. It was going to be another warm day. Some people by the gate were actually fanning themselves. Amongst the locals were ten, maybe fifteen photographers, wobbling on stepladders, leaning over tripods and long-lens cameras. These were not *Stone Harbour Gazette* photographers

68

but looked like paparazzi from the city, or even freelancers for the nationals.

She leaned forward and the sharp sunlight glinted off the metal roof of a van. She scrunched her eyes up. A murmur of excited chatter rippled through the crowd. She stepped left and pressed her head against the wall so she could see the far end of the Cliff Road. Two silver-grey people carriers with blacked-out windows cruised up the hill and turned, crunched across the gravel, gliding to a halt below her window. The actors had arrived.

She spun around, intending to run downstairs again. But someone knocked twice on her door. She stood still in the middle of her room, adrenalin rushing through her body.

There was another knock.

Who would be knocking? Everyone was in the car park, waiting.

'Esther?' said Mum from outside her door. 'Can we come in?'

'Yeah. What? Yeah. I was just going to . . .'

Why was Mum asking to come in like that? It was her habit to knock once then barge right in without waiting for a reply.

The door swung open. Mum and three people she had never seen before walked tentatively into her bedroom.

'This is the room,' said Mum to a wide-hipped woman with green glasses. 'The pretty window there … and the cast-iron fireplace.'

'It's charming. We could take up the carpet, Leo,' the green glasses woman said to the tall man behind her. 'See what's underneath.'

Esther hunched her shoulders and made tight fists with her

hands. Why were these people talking about messing with her room, with her carpet?

'Mum, I …'

'Esther, sweetie, would you pop down and help your dad?' said Mum. 'He's serving coffee and cold drinks to the actors.'

She didn't want to move. She couldn't leave with these people in her room. She raised her hand to her mouth and chewed her thumbnail. 'Um, you won't . . .'

'Now, please.'

She gritted her teeth together. 'You're not going to do stuff

to my room without my permission, are you? It's my room. You wouldn't . . .'

The fourth intruder, a pale, skinny woman, began taking photographs.

Click click … click.

That's it, thought Esther. She may have promised Mum that she'd make a good impression on the crew while they were in the house, but this was unreasonable provocation. She wanted them to leave and leave now, but she couldn't think what to say. If she shouted 'Get out!' at the top of her lungs, like she wanted to, they'd just think she was a moody teenager having a strop. And Mum would be furious. She had to do this the grown-up way. Get out. Find reinforcements.

Dad. Dad would understand.

She stormed out and down the stairs, slamming the 'PRIVATE' door behind her. All those people squeezed into her room had made her panic. But now that she'd left them alone in there, she felt even worse. What might they be doing without her supervision? They could be touching her stuff!

She charged down the last flight of stairs two at a time and flung herself around the corner straight into … a boy! He had a mass of brown hair, pale skin, sad dark eyes rimmed by bruise-like shadows and a slight bump in his nose … and he was gorgeous!

'Hey, watch it!' said the boy.

'S-sorry,' said Esther, her face hot and red with urgency and now embarrassment too.

'Where's the bog?'

'What?'

'The toilet, I'm busting!'

His voice was husky and low. It gave her chills.

'Oh, just there,' she said, pointing at the door behind him. He must be blind and stupid, she thought. Duh! He was standing right in front of a door with a huge 'TOILETS' sign on it!

'Hello, I'm Mike, Mike Armstrong,' said Dad across the lobby. 'Welcome to our home.' He was shaking hands with a group of people over by the door. 'Hello, I'm Mike. Welcome.'

She cringed. Stop talking, Dad. You sound like such a loser.

Dad spotted her at the bottom of the stairs and waved at her. 'And that's my daughter, Esther. We call her Egg.'

She grimaced. Now she wanted to shout at Dad too. She had to press her lips together to stop herself from yelling, 'Don't call me that! Only Max is allowed to call me Egg.'

Max had invented the name. When Esther was born, three-year-old Max had asked where she had come from. When informed that she'd grown from an egg, he had misheard and mashed the two words together, creating Egg-ster.

The actors all turned to look at the red-faced, silent girl at the bottom of the stairs, just a glance of polite acknowledgement, then walked through for a tour of the newly decorated lounge, where the first scene of the day was to be shot. They had more important things to think about than the guest house proprietor's daughter with the eccentric name.

She watched them and tried to remember who they all were. She recognised the director from his visit the previous day, and the older, male actor with the moustache was in something on telly, that weird science fiction series, what was it called? And the woman, who was really beautiful and extremely famous, lived in Los Angeles and was always in the celeb magazines. Dad was now deep in conversation with the stars. This was going to be impossible.

The door opened behind her and the boy shuffled out, wiping his wet hands on the back of his jeans. She looked up into his face. She'd seen him before too, but couldn't recall where. His name was Brian or Ryan or something.

Then a picture popped into her head – a saccharine family movie with a smiling kid. That was him, the kid. What was his name? Not Ryan … Byron … Byron Gale! That was it. He wasn't that smiling kid any more. He'd grown up and he was heavenly. She chewed

excitedly on her thumbnail. Something was fluttering in her stomach. She pictured the black beetle spinning in frantic circles.

Byron brushed his fringe off his pale face and swaggered past her into the lounge. His shoulder muscles flexed and rolled beneath his tight shirt. She wanted him to speak again, to hear the catch in his voice that had raised the hairs on her neck.

Ah, Porphyro! Thy voice was at sweet tremble in mine ear . . .

Byron tilted his head to one side and thrust his thumbs into the belt-loops of his jeans. She couldn't stop watching him.

Give me that voice again, my Porphyro. Oh leave me not in this eternal woe . . .

'Esther.' Someone was saying her name, but it wasn't Byron. Who was interrupting her dream? Go away. Not now.

'Esther.'

She couldn't pull her eyes from Byron's haunting, pallid features.

'Esther!' Dad tapped her on the forehead. 'Are you with us?'

'What?'

'Do you have your brain plugged in?'

'Yeah.' She frowned.

'Well, stop drooling over the actors and lend a hand. We've got a delivery. Come and help me in the kitchen.'

'Daaaaaad,' she hissed, feeling heat rising in her cheeks. Had Byron overheard? She groaned. Oh, please! Don't let him have heard that! I would just die if he did. She darted away across the lobby.

Chapter Nine

She lifted the tray of French sticks and pain au chocolat on to the counter and pushed it angrily against the wall. One minute she was dealing with a personal space violation, and the next she'd forgotten all about it. How had the crisis in her room and the anxiety about being invaded evaporated, just like that? Because her pathetic teen-girl brain had been corrupted by the deadly Byron Gale, that was how. He'd messed with her mind. Byron's deep, dangerous eyes and languid saunter had left her so intoxicated she could hardly remember her own name. But now she had to sober up, remember what was important.

'Dad, they're not going to film in my bedroom, are they?'

'Don't know. Ask your mum. She's in charge of all that,' he said, stacking boxes of eggs and slabs of mozzarella cheese in the big double fridge.

'But I don't want them to touch anything or change stuff. I hate it when someone moves my things.'

'I know. I'm the same. Just tell her. I'm sure she'll understand.'

'But she won't,' she insisted. She was starting to panic again. 'She's only thinking about making more money and sucking up to the celebs. She'll do anything those people ask. She'd pick their noses and wipe their bums, probably.'

'Esther!'

'She would, though. You know what she's like.'

Since signing the contract with the film company, Mum had become increasingly enthusiastic about the arrival of their famous visitors. Now she had some excitement in her life and some *real* glamour, not fake glamour like the bars she frequented with her friends in Silver Sands. This was going to be the sort of hotel she'd always wanted, full of shiny, interesting people, not a sad empty B&B any more.

Dad seemed happier too. He was busy, so had no time to fret over the accounts or to drift about feeling sorry for himself. It was almost like they'd forgotten how to be miserable, forgotten how they'd been over the last few months. Esther had even stopped worrying about treading on eggshells.

'Would it be so bad if they used your room?' Dad asked. 'They'll put it all back like it was, you know ... or better.'

'That's not the point. Nobody consulted me about it and they are INVADING MY PRIVACY!'

She ran up the stairs. She knew she shouldn't have shouted and she was probably being a bit selfish, but why should she have to hide her discomfort? It was so hard. But, she supposed, they were all making sacrifices. Maybe she should try to put up with the disruption. They were only going to be there for a month, after all. And if she made a fuss, she might risk bursting the happiness bubble.

She opened the door marked 'PRIVATE'.

Perhaps if she went out, down to the beach for a while, she'd calm down. She'd text Molly, tell her about the arrival of gorgeous Byron Gale and about how they'd talked to each other, had a real, actual conversation. Molly would be so jealous.

She kicked open her bedroom door and stopped. She slapped her hands over her mouth to stifle a scream. All her furniture had been pushed to the centre of the room; her bed, desk, chair, chest of drawers and even the heavy wardrobe were shunted together, like they were huddled on a sinking raft, circled by hungry sharks. Her computer, books, posters, pen pots, clothes, make-up, jewellery and collection of sunglasses were no longer carefully arranged exactly where she wanted them. They had been swept into a heap and thrown on to the duvet. Her carpet had been rolled up and her footsteps echoed on the cold wooden boards.

But that wasn't the worst thing.

The worst thing was the wall.

The wallpaper above her desk – or where the desk had been – was ripped in a diagonal from the ceiling almost to the fireplace, and hung like a huge peeled banana skin. She retreated and closed the door.

Esther stood up. She'd been sitting for so long on the edge of the bath she had a red stripe across the back of her thighs. She wasn't actually sure how long. Long enough to calm down. Long enough to make the red mark. She rubbed the striped skin and stepped over to the sink. The face that looked back at her in the mirror was pale, grumpy, frowning. And there was a pimple about to erupt on her forehead. She squeezed at it but only succeeded in making it angrier. She shook her hair forward to cover the damage then turned away. Best not to look.

She knew what she had to do. She had to go back, open the door, face what was waiting for her in her bedroom. She'd considered storming downstairs again, making a scene and demanding that her room be returned to its original state, asserting that she wouldn't go back there until it was sorted. But that was what she always did. She ran away from things. And this was her bedroom, her sanctuary. She didn't want strangers to go in there again. She'd have to sort it on her own.

She sniffed, wiped her nose on her sleeve, then pushed her bed against the wall. It had taken almost an hour to put everything back. But even when she'd sat on the floor and forced the wardrobe into the corner with her feet, rolled out her carpet, restuck her posters, straightened her books, plugged in her iPod dock, tilted her bedside lamp to exactly the right angle, lined up her hairbrush, dryer and straighteners, arranged her sunglasses across the top of her mirror and smoothed her pillow a hundred times, there was still something wrong. She stood in the middle of the room, her arms wrapped tightly around her body.

She'd repaired it, put everything back exactly as it was. Why did it still feel wrong, like it was contaminated?

It was the paper.

The torn wallpaper grinned at her. She crossed the room, reached out, took the long tongue in both hands and pulled. It unzipped down the wall and stopped at the fireplace. She yanked again and the heavy cast iron shuddered. The paper ripped away with a crack and something rattled down behind the wall, sounding alarmingly like scurrying mice or a nest of insects flexing hairy limbs. She gasped. She'd made it worse.

She sat on her bed and drew her knees up to her chest. She dropped her face on her knees and draped her arms over her head, but not looking at the rip didn't help. She knew it was there, taunting her. She couldn't ignore it and there was no way she'd be able to sleep in the room tonight. She'd toss and turn with that thing looming above her desk. She raised her head and glared up at the rip, then picked up a book from her bedside table and threw it. There was a swish, a flutter and a thud as the hardback edition of *The Oxford Book of War Poetry* landed, half open, in the fireplace. The cast-iron frame shuddered again. That hadn't made her feel any better. The rip was still there, still smug, like a wonky gloating smile. It had to go.

She stood up, stepped towards the wall and reached out her hand, then stopped. There was something odd that she hadn't noticed before. It wasn't one layer of wallpaper at all, but several stuck together. The guest house was quite old, maybe more than a hundred years, and the rooms would probably have been redecorated many times over. So these must be wallpapers chosen by different owners of the house, stuck one on top of another. She wondered who the many residents of her room might have been.

She remembered the top layer of paper, pale pink with white stripes, which had been there when they'd moved in. She had decided, almost immediately, to make the room her own by covering the walls with two coats of Purple Passion paint, a colour she had taken weeks to choose. Max had made the final choice for her by shutting his eyes and stabbing his finger at the colour chart, landing on the greyish-mauve rectangle. They'd painted the room together, but not before mucking about and making a mess. She smiled at the memory.

They'd put on old clothes and covered the carpet with plastic, then her older brother had picked up a brush, dipped it in the pot and daubed his own name across the wall. She'd pulled another out of the budget brush pack and scrawled

MAX

SMELLS beneath.

Max had retaliated with

EGG IS A YOKE

to which she had answered

HA HA! HILARIOUS

MAX IS ~~COOL~~

A MORON

EGG HAS CHICKEN LEGS

MAX WETS THE BED

Finally, they filled the spaces in between with as many swear words as they could think of, flicking paint all over the floor, the windows and themselves in the process.

Esther stroked her hand over the surface. Their entire painted insult contest was there, under the bruise-coloured surface. She tried to remember where each word had been, but no brush strokes remained. The colour was flat and even. Until she reached the tear.

She scrutinised the ripped layers. The next one down, beneath the purple and the stripes, was mint green with tiny white sprig flowers. Then there was a sort of orange and grey sunflower pattern. She followed the torn edges, tracing the rough surface with her finger. It reminded her of the froth on the waves along the shoreline. She felt further down the wall and looked to see if there was yet another paper beneath. Perhaps it would be a layer that she'd like better than Purple Passion. There *was* a final paper, swirling green leaves then, down by the fireplace, the original pale pink plaster was exposed, like naked skin.

She stepped back. Perhaps if she peeled it back to the plaster it would be OK. She picked tentatively at the ripped edge as if it were a painful scab on her knee. But the tear was so much worse than a knee scab. It was an ugly and disfiguring wound, like a serious accident scar. She dropped her hands. She couldn't just pick at it with her fingernails. The wall needed surgery. Perhaps she should leave it to the film people to sort out after all.

Higher up there was another loose edge, a smaller curled banana skin, so she reached up and pinched the end between her fingers. She pulled. It came away more easily than she'd expected. She staggered, stepped sideways and kicked the base of the fireplace. It made a hollow *thunk* sound and the whole thing shifted. Again, she could hear dust and plaster

falling behind the wall. This time there was a gap. A centimetre-wide split had appeared all the way down the side to the floor. The whole fireplace was loose. She kneeled to take a look. There was something sticking out. It might be an insect, a giant spider's web or parts of a rat's nest. It looked a little like a tail. She shivered and reached into the gap.

Dear Max,

Do you remember I lost that article I cut from the newspaper, the one with the stupid picture of you winning the writing competition and getting a place at uni? Well I found it. It was in my room after all. I must have put it on the ledge above the fireplace and there was a gap (it's always been loose) and it slipped down behind. I found loads of other lost things too, like my skull badge, that orange rubber bracelet you gave me with 'FRAGILE, HANDLE WITH CARE' written on it, a free sachet of apple face scrub, an iTunes gift card I got from Molly and earphones I thought I'd left on the beach. There was other stuff too, lost by someone who lived here before us.

She slipped the orange bracelet on to her left wrist, then placed the envelopes side by side across her bedcover. There were six of them, the colour of sand, dusty, the paper water stained in places, the black ink faded to grey. Six envelopes; five carefully opened, perhaps with a knife, the sixth sealed and the address written in a different hand. Unsent. Unopened. Unread.

She stacked them up in the same order she'd found them behind the fireplace, the unopened one at the bottom, and tapped them gently into a tidy pile with her fingers. Her first instinct had been to read them. But they didn't belong to her. They were secret, personal, and only the recipient should read them. She thought about her letters to Max, and how she'd feel if anyone else were to see what she'd written. The owner of these letters was long gone from the house, perhaps even in their grave, but the contents were still private. They might not have been tied up with a ribbon, like love letters in some soppy romantic novel, but they had probably meant something special to somebody. They'd been kept together and placed for safety on the mantelpiece. The irony of their accidental disappearance made her sad. The fireplace must have been loose like that for a really long time. Not a safe place to put precious things at all.

The mantelpiece no doubt served the same purpose then as it did now, for Esther. It wasn't a proper mantelpiece, just a narrow ledge along the top of the iron fireplace, but it was convenient. It was where she'd line up all her birthday cards and arrange her 'treasures', like the bracelet and the newspaper clipping. She knew how terrible she'd feel if the letters had been hers and she'd lost them behind there.

Who had they been sent to? A child or a servant, perhaps,

in the days when the house was someone's home and not yet a guest house. And why was the sixth one different and unopened? She picked up the top envelope. The address was smudged and difficult to read and the name at the top was partly obscured by brown water stains.

Miss Doro⬤earlow she read.

Pebbleton House, Pebbleton, Dorset.

She flicked the envelopes forward and looked at the last.

Private Frederick Blezzard followed by an address in France.

She went back to the first. She'd just take a quick look inside, see if she could find the name and maybe who'd sent it. Check if it was Frederick. She wouldn't read the whole thing.

10th July 1945

Dearest Dorothea,

There. They'd been sent to a girl who had lived in her room, and her name was Dorothea. Perhaps she'd read a little more. See if she could discover something about her.

This is to let you know we arrived safe and well at the camp. I'm not sure what I had expected but a camp it most certainly is - an enormous field crammed with hundreds of chalk-white tents as far as the eye can see. We'll be under canvas for the duration of our training which some of the lads don't fancy one bit.

The handwriting was swirly and it was really hard to tell the difference between the *e*s and *o*s or between the *h*s and *k*s.

They looked just the same. She flipped the single page over and read the last few lines.

My dearest Dot, I remember your tiny hand resting in my rough paw and dream of golden afternoons at Silver Sands, wind swept strolls on the lighthouse path and those stolen beach kisses. I have these memories to sustain me until I see you again. Would you send a photograph? I should like that very much.

Write soon, my love, and I shall do the same.

Yours forever,

Freddie

Freddie. Freddie must be Frederick. They *were* love letters. Love letters from Freddie Blezzard. Esther's heart fluttered and her cheeks burned as she refolded the paper and slipped it back inside the envelope. She had no right to read them.

Chapter Ten

'Change of plan,' said Mum arranging a breakfast tray. 'They won't need your room any more.'

'But what about my wallpaper?' said Esther, her voice getting louder and higher pitched. 'They can't just leave it like that! You do realise I got absolutely no sleep last night, don't you?'

'Stop shouting, Es. Not here in the kitchen. Calm down and someone will fix it soon.'

'I wasn't shouting, and I am calm.'

Mum held up her hand. 'You're not. You're freaking out. Just decide how you'd like it redecorated. It's simple.'

Esther didn't think it was simple at all. She didn't want new wallpaper. She wanted her old room back, with no wounded wall and no loose fireplace with concealed insect nest.

'I don't want to redecorate. I liked it the way it was.'

'But you can have it back *better* than it was,' said Mum. 'You can get rid of that vile purple paint. I thought you'd be thrilled. Most girls would be. I bet Molly would love to have a brand-new bedroom.'

'Well I wouldn't. And that paint is not vile. I know I said I hated purple but I quite like it now.' She thought about telling Mum that Max's insults written on the wall were the reason she wanted to keep it, but decided Mum would probably think that was weird.

'That's why I pulled off that strip of wallpaper,' said Mum.

'What?' Esther froze. Her veins flooded with ice.

'So they'd have to fix it,' she said with a satisfied smile.

'You mean *you* did it?' Esther pressed her hands into tight fists. 'Why? Why would you do that?' she moaned.

'I thought that's what you'd want.' Mum frowned. 'You're being irrational. Don't you think you might be overreacting? Mmm? I don't know, Es.' She shook her head. 'You're so ungrateful sometimes.'

'Ungrateful? I don't believe this. *You* ripped off my wallpaper and *I'm* the one who's irrational?' Esther boiled with rage. 'You wonder why I'm freaking out. You obviously don't understand me at all. You've never understood me. I hate you! I really hate you!'

She stomped out of the kitchen and slammed the door, hard, behind her. Blood pounded through her hot temples and sweat prickled on her skin. She'd never said anything like that to Mum before. Not even the times when she'd been really upset or tired or hormonal. But Mum deserved it, didn't she? She had ruined her bedroom on purpose, torn Max's purple paintwork. It was the worst thing she'd ever done. Esther really did hate her.

She pushed through a confusion of bodies in the lobby, her vision blurred by anger. Alien shapes seemed to block her escape in all directions through a building that no longer resembled her home. Raucous crew clogged the dining room and mechanical beasts with metal limbs huddled ominously below the stairs. There was no peace, no space to think. Where could she find sanctuary? She stood on the edge of the chaos, waiting for a break in the traffic as if preparing to cross a busy highway. She took a step, faltered, and finally decided to run for it. She dashed for the front door and stumbled out into white morning heat.

She blinked away her sun blindness. Outside was no calmer and no more familiar. The people out here were just as preoccupied, and those that weren't dashing about were oddly dressed. There were small girls in frilled smocks playing with boys in brown boots. Nearby, a woman leaning against a van held a cardboard coffee cup against the crisp white front of a long apron. And above the heads of the milling crew, a strange exotic bird danced towards her. The crowd parted and Esther saw that it wasn't a bird. It was a bouquet of grey feathers adorning a hat. The hat fluttered closer and the face beneath came into focus, the famous Hollywood actress.

'You OK, hon?' she asked in a twinkling half-English, half-American voice.

'Uh . . . um, y-yeah,' Esther stuttered. She could feel the anger in her cheeks becoming embarrassment again. The actress looked as if she was going to ask her something else, which filled Esther with mild panic. She wasn't calm enough to attempt a conversation with anyone, let alone a movie star. How could she get away without seeming rude or crazy?

She had her hands in her pockets and felt the letters on the left side and her phone on the right. She pulled out the phone.

'Oh, that's my phone ringing,' she said, glancing up at the actress. 'Um, I've been waiting for this call. It's quite important. Will you excuse me?' She put the silent, lifeless phone to her ear and walked away, darting quickly behind a van.

Out of sight, her face crumpled into a horrified cringe. That had been awful, so unconvincing! Why on earth had she said that? It had sounded like a line from a film, the sort of thing a high-powered lawyer would say, not a fifteen-year-old surf girl. She groaned and leaned against the cool side of the vehicle.

The back of the van was open, its sliding door rolled up

into the roof and its hydraulic platform, for lifting things in and out, half raised. Esther peered in. Apart from a heap of grey blankets and coils of blue ropes, it was empty, a dark echoing cavern. She climbed on to the platform, which swayed and rattled, then stepped up into the van and crawled a little way inside. Now hidden, she sat and crossed her legs. She looked down at her phone, wishing it would ring or buzz or do something to magically transport her somewhere else. Maybe she could call someone to come and save her? She'd text Molly, arrange to meet on the beach, tell her about her torn wallpaper nightmare and the discovery of the letters. Molly would calm her down, offer solutions. Her thumbs fluttered over the buttons.

Beach?

Molly's reply took a few seconds.

Working @ mum's shop. Off at 6. Mx

Esther blew out her cheeks and sighed. What would she do now?

A shadow fell across the dented metal platform in front of her as a dark shape appeared around the side of the van. A figure approached, silhouetted against the bright sunlight.

'You sound annoyed,' said the dark shape.

She looked up. The shape was a soldier wearing a sludge-green uniform, belted and tight fitting. His face was in shade.

'Oh, sorry! I didn't . . . I mean…'

She probably wasn't allowed to be inside the van. She jumped to her feet and stumbled down on to the platform. It wobbled again and sent her staggering to the edge, where she jumped. The soldier reached out his arm and, without thinking, she grabbed his sleeve to steady her landing. The fabric felt rough and prickly in her hand, like the seats on the bus, and she thought how uncomfortable it must be for him to be buttoned to the neck like that on such a warm day.

The soldier chuckled. 'You're not very good at steps, are you?'

She knew that voice, knew that chuckle. It was Byron Gale.

'Boyfriend?' he asked.

'What?' Esther swallowed. Her insides were swirling so much she thought she might throw up.

'Boyfriend trouble?' he asked again, glancing down at the phone that was still clasped in her hand.

'Oh . . . um, no . . . I don't have . . . I mean, my . . . Mol-Molly . . . my friend . . .' She stopped talking and stuffed the phone into her pocket. Shut up, Esther! You're sounding like a moron! What was she trying to say, anyway? Should she have just said yes, that was my boyfriend and I just broke up with him? Might Byron take pity on her, ask her out to cheer her up? She shook her head. Unlikely.

'You been shown around costume or the make-up trailer yet?'

'What?' Why had he mentioned make-up? Had he spotted her pimple? She grabbed her fringe and pulled it down over her eye.

'Come and meet Lewis and Carrie in make-up. When I get bored listening to their gossip, you can tell me about your friend.'

'O-Ok.' She still wasn't sure what he was proposing, but followed him anyway, on shaking legs, around to the other side of the van and over to a long white trailer near the garden hedge. 'HAIR & MAKE-UP' announced a sign on the door.

Chapter Eleven

Esther tucked her feet under her, wedged herself in the corner of the sofa inside the make-up trailer and watched the artists at work. She was still shaking, almost sick with excitement, and using all her strength to appear calm. She tried to act like being invited to a make-up trailer by a gorgeous movie star was an everyday occurrence.

Byron had thrown his long limbs into a chair in front of a wide mirror surrounded by a glowing halo of lights. Below his bright reflection was an altar laid out with numerous bottles, jars, tubs and palettes – the tools of the illusionist.

'Mm, you been partying till the small hours, eh?' said the young man who began dabbing Byron's nose with a wedged sponge.

Byron beamed his staggering smile at him. 'Always. Partying is in my contract.'

'Yeah, well your contract says you've got to look like a fresh-faced teenager today.' He laughed.

'I know you'll do your best, Lewis.' Byron clicked his tongue, made a two-finger salute with both hands as if they were a pair of pistols, then kicked his feet out and spun the chair around in a full circle. Lewis stepped back and tutted.

At the other end of the trailer, a red-haired girl appeared through a sliding door with what looked like a severed head tucked under her arm. This must be Carrie, Esther thought. Carrie approached the mirror and smiled at Lewis. She cleared a space and put the severed head down on the altar in the bright pool of light, where Esther was able to see that the ashen face was in fact polystyrene and the brown hair perched on top was a wig.

'Have we decided?' she asked Byron. 'Wig or cut?'

'Cut,' said Byron. 'But only the back. Leave my fringe.'

'Mmmm.' Carrie half closed her eyes and tilted her head. 'I'll see what I can do. I suppose I could flatten it somehow.'

Byron rubbed his fingers vigorously over his head, fluffing his mass of hair in all directions.

Carrie sighed. 'You've got so much of it. That's the problem.' She drew a pair of narrow, pointed scissors from her pocket and snapped them in the air.

'Just the back,' said Byron.

'You have to look like a soldier in 1915, you know,' said Carrie.

'Yeah. Short at the back. You can gel the rest.'

'OK. Just the back.'

Esther watched as Lewis dabbed and smoothed then flourished brushes, swept and flicked. Then Carrie took over and draped a rustling black cape around Byron's khaki shoulders. She began to comb and snip. Esther tried to concentrate on their conversation. The three of them were discussing all the films Byron had been in, the actors Lewis and Carrie had worked with and their mutual acquaintances in the film business. It was just the sort of juicy movie-star gossip the celeb mags were full of, but Esther's initial excitement had faded. Lewis and Carrie were just like her mum. Mum seemed to think that actors were more important than ordinary people. Just because they were good at pretending didn't make them special. Pretending is easy, Esther thought. People pretend all the time. Mum and Dad pretend that everything is fine when it isn't. Gull pretends he's a Pebbleton gangster. Molly pretends she's some sort of glamorous Parisian intellectual.

Although she had to admit, Byron was not at all like ordinary people, not like any of the boys she knew, anyway. There was no question about it, even with his hair flattened and wearing an ugly sludge-green uniform he was gorgeous. Despite this, watching his gorgeous hair being brushed and his gorgeous nose being dabbed was actually quite boring. As the minutes ticked away, Esther's mind began to wander. She started to think about the letters in her pocket.

Although she had decided that they were secret and private and she wasn't going to read them, her resolve was weakening. When Byron had appeared beside the van and asked her if the text had been 'boyfriend trouble', she'd wondered what it would be like to get a romantic letter from a boyfriend instead of a load of rubbish texts. Texts were never romantic. Not even with hundreds of xs and hearts.

Letters took longer to write and longer to arrive. She wondered how many days each of Freddie's letters had travelled to reach Pebbleton. And where he had written them. And why he had gone there. All the answers were probably in the letters somewhere, here, in her pocket, just waiting to be opened, unfolded and read. Perhaps it wouldn't be so bad if she just took another peek.

She eased them out of her pocket and selected the first one again. She looked for a postmark, but the smudges near the stamp were unreadable. So she drew out the letter and smoothed it open against her thigh.

10th July 1915

Dearest Dorothea,

This is to let you know we arrived safe and well at the camp. I'm not sure what I had expected but a camp it most certainly is - an enormous field crammed with hundreds of chalk-white tents as far as the eye can see. We'll be under canvas for the duration of our training which some of the lads don't fancy one bit.

He was at a training camp. What sort of training camp and why were they sleeping in tents? Esther remembered when the big field across the road from Teasel Wood had been filled with tents during the Smuggler's Rock Festival. The tents hadn't been chalk white, though. They had been green and orange and blue and pink and black and red. There had been tiny single-person tents that sprung out of bags fully formed and there had been enormous exotic-looking yurts that had taken a day to erect. Esther suspected that Freddie's camp looked very different, but she couldn't quite picture it.

The food is good and our training has given us enormous appetites, though last night's apple pie wasn't a patch on my ma's. We've not yet been measured for our uniforms but I fear I may need a larger size.

We shall miss the Pebbleton treasure hunt this year and I shall miss searching with you, my dearest Dot.

She shivered with delight. The village still had a

treasure hunt every summer. It was a traditional thing, commemorating a time when smugglers were said to have used Pebbleton's cellars and boathouses to hide their contraband. For hundreds of years the village had celebrated a weekend of carnival every August. There were street parties and beach barbecues and everyone dressed up as pirates to run around the fields and cliff paths following clues to hidden prizes. Esther and her brothers had been eager participants when they were younger, putting on striped sailor tops and drawing curly moustaches on their faces. In recent years enthusiasm for the event had been dampened by cynicism. The older kids began to devise acts of sabotage, deciding that subverting the hunt was more fun than taking part. They'd beat the smaller kids to the hidden sweets and toys and replace them with apple cores, dead birds, half-empty packets of laxative gum and notes that read 'Treasure Seized by THE REBELLION'. This year, she'd heard, a decision had been made to ban anyone over twelve from taking part.

I remember your tiny hand resting in my rough paw and dream of golden afternoons at Silver Sands, wind swept strolls on the lighthouse path and those stolen beach kisses. I have these memories to sustain me until I see you again. Would you send a photograph? I should like that very much.

Write soon, my love, and I shall do the same.

Yours forever,

Freddie

Esther folded the paper in half and slipped it back into the envelope. Did Dot ever send that photo? Would Freddie fit into his uniform? She put the first letter to the back of the pile and picked up the second. Her hand froze in mid air as a chill ran through her body. Uniform? What uniform? She looked up at Byron's reflection in the mirror. Carrie had smoothed his wild hair and trimmed the ragged strands that had trailed down his neck. He looked so different, almost unrecognisable. She gasped and tugged the second letter out of the envelope. The first had been written in July 1915 and the second in September of the same year. 1915! Freddie was being measured for a soldier's uniform. He was at a camp where he was training to go to war. The First World War!

'What's up?' said Byron's reflection. 'You seen a ghost?'

'Y-you look so . . . different, that's all.'

He nodded. 'What's that?' he asked, pointing at her chest.

Esther still had the second letter in her raised hand. 'Oh, this? Um, a letter I found. Well, six letters actually. I think they might be from...' She paused. She shouldn't have blurted that out. It was bad enough having read Freddie's letter when she'd decided not to. Now she'd almost told Byron about them. She slid them back into her pocket.

'Might be what?'

'Nothing.'

Byron raised his eyebrows. 'Uh?'

She fidgeted. She didn't like him staring at her like that. It made her self-conscious, uncomfortable. She tilted her head down so her face was hidden behind her hair. She wriggled and unhooked her feet then swung her legs round and began to stand up. 'Um, I just remembered I'm supposed to be somewhere.' She stared at the door.

'OK. See ya later?'

Esther shuffled towards the exit, mumbling agreement and chewing on her mangled thumbnail. She fumbled with the awkward door handle and jumped when the latch clicked and the door swung outwards, launching her down the steps faster than she'd anticipated.

'Careful on those steps!' Byron yelled as Esther landed and regained her balance. His husky laugh tumbled out of the door after her. She felt sick and cold, just like the time she fainted in a particularly long school assembly and hit her head on the edge of a chair in front of the whole school. She hoped she wasn't about to do it again. Humiliating herself twice in front of him was bad enough, now she'd done it three times. *Three!* She couldn't survive fainting as well. She pulled up her hood and crept away to search for solitude.

She found it upstairs, in Max's tiny room at the end of the top-floor corridor. Max's room was quiet, safe and currently unoccupied. Nobody would think to look for her there. It was the perfect place to read the other letters.

Dearest Dotty,

There is no sign of an end to this training, nor to the rain, which pours down day and night. Our kit is so damp we should sprout mushrooms. If we don't get to France soon, the war will be over while we're still trapped in this field, sunk to our knees in mud.

The only compensation is that, at last, we now look like soldiers. I'm so proud to wear this uniform. Young women smile, old men doff their caps and I've lost count of the beers we've been bought. There is a photographer in the town, so in the next rare hour away from the camp I shall pay him a visit to prove to you how straight my back has become and how high my chin. I treasure your picture, which lies in my breast pocket pressed against my heart.

She sighed and leaned back. Dotty *did* send a photograph. And Freddie got his uniform. What would happen next? She had four more letters. Freddie would go to war, leaving behind the girl he loved. He'd write about what it was like in France. But why did Dorothea not send that last one to him? Esther chewed the raw skin around her left thumbnail and winced at the pain. Did Dotty meet someone else and write the letter to break up with Freddie then chicken out of sending it? Did it get lost before

she'd had a chance to take it to the post box? Or did something else happen?

'Esther!'

Someone was calling her name, and had been calling for some time. Would they guess she was in Max's room? She hoped not. She wanted to read the other letters without interruption.

'Esther!'

It was Mum. Esther jumped, anxious for a moment that she might have forgotten something important. What time was it? How long had she been sitting on Max's bed, reading and day-dreaming about Freddie and Dorothea? Could it already be time to begin her lunchtime shift in the kitchen?

She put the second letter away and opened the third.

'Esther?'

'Urgh! Go away!' she growled, exasperated. Her eyes darted over the page. Freddie's handwriting had become a scrawl. He'd written this one in a hurry and in pencil.

. . . two days' leave . . . sorry not to see you, my dearest Dot. You'd think me quite changed, not the shy boy you once knew . . . We Pebbleton lads are keen to get to France and teach Fritz a lesson . . packing our kit . . .

'Esther, you're wanted in the kitchen. You don't come in the next five minutes, we'll give your job to someone else, someone who really wants it.'

Mum must have been standing at the top of the stairs. She was enunciating her lines like an actress projecting her voice to the back of a theatre. There was a pause, then she mumbled

108

something. Another pause. Esther held her breath. Her phone beeped and vibrated.

You wanted this job. Kitchen 5mins or sacked. Mum

Esther waited until Mum had retreated downstairs, then crept back down the corridor, changed into her apron and trudged reluctantly to the kitchen.

Chapter Twelve

Esther leaned back against the cold stone and raised her phone.

Mol, better B quick if you want to see him. Crowds of Byron fans already. Save U spot on memorial steps. E

She punched send, then looked up at the bizarre spectacle unfolding across the village green. The streets had been cleared of cars and most of the houses that faced the crossroads had been repainted in drab shades of green and brown, their gardens replanted and bins removed. Old-fashioned shop fronts and street lamps had been erected in place of neon signs and plastic bollards. The newsagent had been transformed into a quaint corner shop and the Black Lamb pub had lost the ten-metre banner promoting 'BIG SCREEN SATELLITE SPORT'. Even the yellow lines outside the library had been covered with a layer of grit. By removing or disguising all signs of the twenty-first century, Pebbleton had magically slipped back a hundred years.

From her perch on the war memorial steps, Esther had a perfect view of the film people in front of the library and the gathering crowds of locals and tourists taking photos of the empty high street and the glinting strip of camera track that sliced it down the middle. Nothing had happened yet apart from the occasional appearance of a member of the film crew traversing the centre of the ghost village, stepping over the track and jabbering into a walkie-talkie.

Once again they had started early. In this second week of filming, Esther was getting used to the routine, which began at dawn with the sleepy crew in padded jackets moving equipment about, and ended at dusk with frantic activity to catch the fading daylight. She had been surprised at first; not by the long days, nor by padded jackets in July, but by how tedious it all was. Making movies was not what she'd expected at all. She'd concluded it was the most boring business in the universe.

Every scene would take hours to set up, and the cast had to wait in full costume, sometimes in a huddle of chairs under an awning and sometimes frozen in position on set, until everything was just right. Then all of a sudden the director would announce he was ready and they'd 'go for a take'. Silence would fall, the scene would be shot and then the process would start again. Some scenes were filmed over and over because the light had changed or the director wanted to try something different.

This morning's outside shoot involved a lot of extras who had been dressed in their uncomfortable Edwardian clothes and wearing full make-up since before breakfast. Esther stood up to see if she could spot Gulliver among them. Today was her brother's first appearance on set, and he'd been unbearable, taunting her for days with rehearsal anecdotes and with assertions of his own imminent stardom. There was no sign of Byron either, and it was him she'd really come to see. It would be Molly's first chance to meet him too. Her mum's shop was doing a lot of extra business since the film people had moved into the village, so Molly was helping out there every other day. Esther couldn't wait to prove to her that she and Byron had become good friends.

Since that first morning she had made a point of 'accidentally' meeting the young actor as often as she could – at breakfast, or outside the costume van, where they would exchange a few words about the sweltering weather or what ugly outfit Byron had been required to put on. But not today. His mop of brown hair and pallid face were nowhere to be seen.

Esther sighed and was about to slump back against the memorial when she saw something she did recognise: the black sling. The bruised boy was standing in the crowd just a few metres away. He turned his head and she delayed dipping her eyes just long enough for his gaze to meet hers. She blinked and blushed and he hesitantly raised his hand. She smiled back, then turned away, and when she looked up again he was coming towards her.

'Hello.'

'Hi.' She wobbled nervously on the edge of the stone plinth. 'How's your arm?'

'Watch out, mate!' said a voice behind her. 'She has a problem with steps.'

'Huh?' Esther swung around and immediately lost her balance, falling back against a buttress. She looked up at the

patch of shadow above her. A dark figure was sitting on a wall in the shade of an overhanging branch.

'Told you!' The figure laughed.

It was Byron Gale. The fans only a few metres away hadn't spotted him hidden up there beneath the horse chestnut tree.

'Oh . . . um . . . yeah, I suppose I do,' she stammered. She smiled, but her insides were dissolving. Of course she didn't have a problem with steps! That was ridiculous! She had a problem with him, with Byron. It was his fault she couldn't control her body when he was around. That smile and those eyes turned her brain to mush and her limbs to water. She'd be able to manage steps just fine if he'd only stop surprising her like that and smiling at her and being so utterly edible.

'You . . . you're that actor?' said the boy with the sling.

Esther turned. She'd forgotten he was there. How did Byron manage to do that to her every time? One minute she was talking to a really cute boy, the next she was under Byron's spell again.

'Yep,' said Byron, leaping down beside her.

The boy was already stepping backwards. 'Um, hi . . . I mean, bye. Gotta go.' He raised his hand again, this time in farewell, and Esther felt a tug of disappointment as he melted back into the crowd. Byron had scared him away.

'You look just like your brother,' said Byron.

Esther frowned. Her brother? How did Byron know Max? Then the memory that she had two brothers shot a blush of shame through her cheeks. 'Oh, right, Gulliver?' She frowned. 'I do not look like Gulliver. He's . . . he's a . . . a . . .'

'An ape?' said Molly, trotting around the memorial and climbing the steps to join them.

'Exactly,' said Esther.

'Vile swamp beast?' Molly suggested.

'Smile ape swap . . . what she said.' The liquidised state of Esther's brain had completely removed her ability to speak.

'*Bonjour,* I'm Molly,' sang Molly, tilting her head to the side and grinning at Byron.

'Hell-o, Mollee,' Byron sang back. 'Like your T-shirt.'

'Oh, really, this old thing?' Molly looked down at her pink 'hot dog' T-shirt with the famous dog-on-a-skateboard logo stretched tight across her ample chest. Esther knew her friend was lying. The T-shirt wasn't old, it was brand new. Just two days before, they'd both gone over on the ferry to the opening of the super-cool surf shop in Silver Sands. Esther had bought a 'hot dog' T-shirt too, though hers was grey and wasn't quite as snug as Molly's.

Byron grinned back, then reached into his waistcoat pocket and pulled out a vibrating smartphone. 'Looks like I'm needed on set,' he announced, and thrust the phone back into his pocket.

It wasn't until that moment, when Byron stepped down from the war memorial and began to walk away from them, that Esther noticed how he was dressed. It wasn't the khaki uniform she'd seen him wearing so often up at the house. Today he was in old-fashioned civilian clothes: dark corduroy trousers, brown lace-up boots, a cream collarless shirt and black waistcoat.

She recalled the long explanation that Gull had delivered at breakfast. The film was being shot out of sequence, meaning some of the end of the story had already been completed while the opening scenes hadn't. Today they would shoot the

part where the
lead character, Tom,
and his friends decide to enlist in the army
and go off to fight in the war. Gull would be playing one of
the younger boys in the village.

Esther ignored Molly, who was swooning and twittering
something about being in lust and wanting to be the mother
of Byron's babies. She watched the fans swoop on him,
jabbing phones and cameras in his face and demanding that
he sign his name on bits of paper. Finally they let him go and
he joined the other actors and extras taking up their positions
in the street. The director, who'd removed his padded jacket,
though not his flappy-eared ski hat, put his arm around
Byron's shoulders and the two paced back and forth for a

few minutes, Byron nodding and the director waving his free hand about.

The director retreated to the shade of the awning. Byron sat in a chair and Carrie, the girl from the hair and make-up trailer, slapped something gloopy, gel or wax, on to his unruly hair, smoothing it against his head. He stood, walked a little way along the street, then someone shouted, 'Quiet, please!' and the onlookers fell silent. Byron blew out his cheeks and looked down at the pavement, and when he looked up again his face had changed. He'd become Tom, a teenage boy in 1915. Esther was mesmerised. The whole mysterious alchemy of film-making was happening right in front of her.

The camera, which was mounted on a sort of trolley, had been rolled to the far end of the high street, and as it was dragged slowly back towards them along the track, a group of men – some in uniform but most dressed as if they'd just recently been ploughing a field, wrapping sausages in the butcher's or hunched over ledgers in an accountants' office – marched together around the corner. It reminded her of Freddie's first letter.

I remember your tiny hand resting in my rough paw and dream of golden afternoons at Silver Sands, wind swept strolls on the lighthouse path and those stolen beach kisses.

Had Freddie been a clerk or farm boy like these lads? Were his rough paws the result of labouring in the Pebbleton fields or of hauling ropes in sailboats off the coast? Had he and his mates marched through the village just like this? Esther's heart thumped in time with their boots.

A cheer went up from the costumed extras and smocked children waved tiny Union flags above their heads. As the camera swivelled and swept past the faces of the crowd, it reached Tom and his four friends. Esther was too far away to hear their lines, but she could see their faces and their expressions. Byron was only acting, pretending, but, as she watched, she found that she was able to imagine what Tom, his character, was feeling: excitement, pride and fear all at the same time. The men marching past had just enlisted in the army. They were the husbands, fathers and elder brothers of the proud, flag-waving villagers. Even without hearing the actors' words she knew from the straightness of their backs and the set of their jaws that Tom and his friends were filled with envy and patriotic fervour. These boys were not going to let a trivial thing like age prevent them from going to war.

It was thrilling. Adrenalin rushed around her body. She was no longer just thinking about Freddie. If she'd been alive in 1915, like Dorothea, these boys could have been her own friends, her own brothers, marching past. Her eyes itched and a lump formed in her throat. And Byron was an amazing actor. He was so believable, so real. Now she had an even bigger crush on him.

Dear Max,

Gull made his debut on film today, waving a flag. Tough job. I still can't believe he's actually getting paid for that.

The film is a lot more interesting than I thought. The main character is a boy called Tom, played by Byron Gale, who was in that kids movie years ago. Remember? We watched it a million times until the DVD wore out. It drove Dad crazy when we quoted lines from it all the time. In fact, I think he may have scratched the disc on purpose so he didn't have to listen to us screeching the theme tune any more. Well, anyway, Tom is only seventeen, which is too young to enlist in the army, but he and his friends go to a recruiting office in a different town and they lie and say they are older and all except one of them is believed and they go off to fight in France. When his mum, who is being played by Hollywood legend Ernestine Hardy (I know!!), finds out what he's done, she's really proud at first. Then, when she hears the truth about the carnage in the trenches, she tries to have him sent home for being underage and starts this sort of campaign. I'm not sure what happens at the end because they are filming everything in the wrong order and it's quite difficult to put the whole story together.

Anyway, Byron and Ernestine are brilliant actors and Gull is rubbish but that hasn't stopped him rampaging about like he's a celebrity. What a freak! I wish you were here. You'd know exactly what to say to make him stop.

I wish you could see how Mum and Dad have changed too. Dad's a lot more like a human being these days and I don't think Mum has time for Chardonnay.

I've been reading those letters. I know I said I wouldn't, but I kind of need to know what happened to Freddie, if he made it home. If you were here you could help me find out. I don't want to share them with anyone else.

Love and all that other stuff,

Egg-ster x

Dearest Dotty,

This is the first chance I've had to write home since those two days' leave. I was sorry not to see you, my dearest Dot. What terrible bad luck that you should be away from the village, visiting your cousins, that same week. Ma cried when she saw my uniform. You'd think me quite changed, not the shy boy you once knew. I'm so glad we are on our way at last. We Pebbleton lads are keen to get to France and teach Fritz a lesson.

We spent last night packing our kit, and before we knew it the sun was up and we were on the Dover train.

Will Sapsworth was as sick as a dog all the way across the Channel. We all agreed it was a good thing he didn't join the navy.

This third letter, written with a blunt pencil, was harder to decipher.

We slept in a barn and tried out our meagre French on the locals. Jimmy Swain has a French aunt so he taught us a few phrases, but I doubt my ability to purchase ribbon or a hatpin will come in very useful here!

Esther folded it in half and slipped it back inside the envelope. He was in France and getting nearer to the front, nearer to danger, with each letter. She rolled over on her bed and listened to the hubbub of voices in the house below. She wasn't ready to read the others. Not yet. Not here.

Chapter Thirteen

Esther was stressed out. She'd concluded that the provision of personal space was top of her list of 'Essential Conditions for Good Mental Health of a Fifteen-Year-Old Girl'. And today, once again, personal space was pretty much impossible to find. The beach was a battlefield, the whole guest house was stuck in a bizarre Hollywood time warp, her bedroom was wounded and even Max's room didn't feel much like a sanctuary since 'The Invasion'. Her kitchen job was torture, more exhausting than a TV chef contest, and she needed somewhere to chill, to zone out, away from the chaos. There *was* one other place she could try.

After the frenzy of preparing breakfast had died down and the chef had released her from her shift, she ripped off her apron, dashed upstairs and thrust the six envelopes into

her sweatshirt pocket. She left the guest house by the side door and ducked down her secret escape route. The alleyway seemed to get narrower each time she used it. She pushed out through the hedge at the far end, brushing cobwebs from her hair, into a stream of people. She was shocked by their numbers and at the unnecessarily large quantities of holiday paraphernalia they seemed to be carrying down to the beach. The tourists had been clogging the ferry and filling the car parks since daybreak. They'd not been drawn there purely by the continuing glorious weather. Word had spread outside the village that a film company had been shooting nearby, and that movie stars were in the vicinity.

Most of the people were turning left where the path branched, heading towards the dunes, but Esther took the right-hand fork, away from the crowds, down to the cliffs and a line of old fishing shacks where Dad kept his sailboats. The ancient boathouse had been one of the outbuildings included

in the purchase of Pebbleton Beach Guest House and Dad had claimed it for himself, buying a small dinghy at auction during their first summer as hotel owners. She shivered as the path dipped into the shaded space between the buildings then opened out on to a concrete ramp. Her eyes took a while to adjust to the morning sun glinting on the water. Dad's was the second boathouse on the slipway. They were solidly built of stone, brick and weatherboard, each with a large workshop at the front for the boats and storerooms intended for ropes and nets at the back.

The wide double doors of Dad's were propped open, so Esther climbed the slope and peered into the gloom. Dad was hunched in the smaller of his two sailing dinghies, winding a rope around his bent arm, hand to elbow.

'Hello, my little Omelette,' he said. 'How are you doing?'

''Kay.' She shrugged. 'Are you going out?' she asked, nodding towards the sea.

'Maybe tomorrow. Came down for some peace and quiet, really.'

'Me too,' said Esther.

'Slightly crazy up there, isn't it?'

Esther nodded and gave a half-smile but knew it wasn't convincing.

'Wanna help me with these?' Dad released the coil of rope and dropped it on the deck.

She shrugged and ran her fingers along the edges of the envelopes in her pocket. She'd been hoping that Dad wouldn't be moping in here; that he'd gone for a sail around the lighthouse, which he often did when Mum or the guest house started turning him into Zombie Dad. He'd zigzag to the

cove, drop a line over the side, catch a mackerel or two, and sail home slightly less zombie and more like Dad.

There was a sort of attic in the boathouse roof where he'd installed an old camp bed and stacked dusty piles of sailing and boat design magazines. She'd thought, if he was out, she might climb up there, crash on the camp bed, see if she could pluck up the courage to read the remaining letters and decide what to do about them. But the sea was calm, not quite enough breeze for sailing, so Dad was loafing inside.

Her plan frustrated, she casually circled the dinghies and began picking up random tools from Dad's workbench. Alongside the usual ropes, oars, sails and gear, Dad had furnished his sanctuary with an eccentric collection of maps and sailing memorabilia, together with the products of his other hobby, building miniature model boats. He had a flotilla of them arranged on a windowsill, including several which, implausibly, sat inside small bottles.

It was a clever technique. Esther had watched him do it once. He'd make the tiny boat so the masts and sails could fold down to the width of the bottle-neck, then, once inside, by pulling on a sequence of threads, the boat would unfurl to fill the glass.

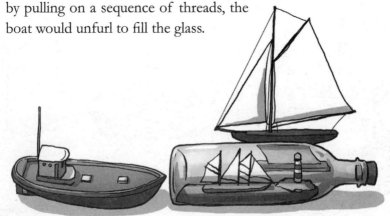

She picked up one of the bottles and brought it up close to her face so the boat appeared almost as big as the dinghy Dad was sitting in. This was her favourite. It looked older and she wasn't sure if Dad had made this one. He sometimes found a worthy addition to his collection in sailing-themed antique shops in nearby villages. This specimen was a pretty black sailboat with a dark red mainsail and spinnaker, and it reminded her that she'd not been out in a boat since Max had left.

Max was the true sailor of the family. Since they'd moved to the coast they'd all learned new skills. Dad found that he liked to design and build models, Mum swam (and now drank) like a fish, Esther and Gull were great on a surfboard, but Max was the natural under sail. He seemed to be able to guess exactly what the wind was about to do and had a reputation for winning races around Smuggler's Rock. Max excelled at everything: sailing, sport, school, sneaking girlfriends into his room.

Esther smiled, then caught sight of a face behind the boat, distorted by the glass. She dropped her hands a little so she could see more clearly. It was a framed photo of Max teaching a tiny Gull how to row. Next to it, fastened to the wall, was one of Mum taken the week they'd moved to Pebbleton, wearing a wetsuit and trying to surf for the first, and last, time. Below Mum's photo, a heart and a circle had been carved into the brickwork. Both shapes had smooth edges, as if many fingers had traced them. They must have been carved a long time ago, she thought. Some sort of secret love message, perhaps.

She put the bottle back in the flotilla and scanned the other photographs. They weren't all of the family. Some were much older, black and white photos of the beach and the boathouse, taken years ago, probably before she, Gull, Max or even Dad was born.

'Dad?'

'Mm?'

'Who lived in our house before us?'

'You mean who did we buy it from?'

'Yeah. Well . . . no. Before it was a hotel it was a house, right?'

'I suppose so,' said Dad, releasing the coil of rope from his arm and securing it over a cleat. 'It's been a guest house for quite a long time, though. Before the war, I think.'

'You mean the second war?' Esther asked.

'Yep. Not the First World War. That was—'

'Nineteen fourteen to nineteen eighteen, like in the film,' Esther announced. At least she'd learned something in history lessons and reading those gloomy war poems.

Dad nodded and picked up another length of rope.

Esther flicked nervously at the edges of the envelopes with her fingernail. 'You don't know who lived here back then, do you, in about 1915, when it was just Pebbleton House?'

'No, but I suppose it could well have been a family just like in the film.'

She was itching to tell Dad he was right, that there was a real girl called Dorothea and her boyfriend was a real soldier called Freddie and she'd found their letters. But then he'd ask questions and she didn't know how she would explain about being too scared to read the ones sent from France because of what might be in them. They'd studied the First World War in Year Eight. She knew a bit about what had happened to the soldiers in the trenches and it was awful. She remembered what Wilfred Owen had described in his poems too. She could imagine the horror of the mud, the machine guns, the barbed wire and the poison gas. Freddie would have experienced all of that and he'd probably written about it.

Then there was the final unsent, unopened letter, the one addressed to *Private Frederick Blezzard*, that filled her with dread. Sharing all that with Dad would be tricky. It was better to keep it as her secret. Better to deal with it on her own. Perhaps there would be a way to find out what happened to Freddie without reading the letters.

'There,' said Dad. He was leaning over the side of the boat, his arm reaching out, the rope dangling from his elbow.

'What?'

'That picture.' He pointed at the wall of photographs. 'That picture of the cove was taken around that time, I think, the old fisherman with the huge boots and beard. There are loads of them at the museum, you know. Not boots or beards.' He sniggered. 'Old photographs of the village. I expect they'll have some of Pebbleton House as it was a hundred years ago.'

Esther stopped fidgeting with the envelopes. The hairs on her arms stood to attention beneath her sleeve. She stared at the photo of the bearded fisherman standing beside his boat in the cove, her heart beating fast. Of course. Why hadn't she thought of the museum? It was obvious. That was where her search for Freddie and Dotty should start.

She blinked. How long did she have to pretend to look at the fisherman? she wondered.

'I've been meaning to go to that exhibition myself,' said Dad. 'I guess next time I need some peace, I'll sneak off and check it out.' He chuckled quietly to himself and began to wind the rope again.

'Mm,' Esther mumbled. She wasn't listening. She was backing towards the door.

'Hey,' said Dad. 'You off already? I thought you were going to help me.'

She smiled. 'Nah. Things to do, places to go, people to see.'

Dad's face fell. 'OK. Bye then.'

Outside, Esther began to jog.

Chapter Fourteen

Inside the Pebbleton Museum, Esther didn't know where to start. She wandered from room to room in the cool gloom, her eyes drifting over numerous badly lit glass cases of dirty coins, dusty Roman pots and framed maps. She was considering a return to the entrance to ask someone where she might find photographs when something bright glinted, green and purple, across the room. It twinkled at her in a narrow ribbon of sunlight and seemed to beckon her over.

Full on this casement shone . . . something, something . . . *and threw warm gules on* . . . something. Oh, I forget. That was Keats. I think.

In a glass case near the window was a necklace, a pretty but modest arrangement of pearls with faceted gemstones in mauve and pale green, resting on a pad of grey velvet.

Behind it was an old black and white photograph, an elegant woman wearing the necklace. She had a long neck and a wide cushion of dark hair piled on top of her head. She looked about Mum's age, and the necklace suited her. Esther leaned forward to read the caption.

'A necklace of amethyst, pearl and peridot commissioned for his wife by . . .'

Her body jolted.

'. . . Charles Dearlove of Pebbleton House.'

Dorothea Dearlove must have been related to Charles Dearlove. Were Charles and the woman in the picture Dotty's parents, perhaps? There were more photographs across the

wall above the case and Esther moved quickly from one to another, experiencing a tingle of recognition as she was confronted by places she knew. There was the cove, and that was the lighthouse. And was that the centre of the village before the war memorial was built? There was a picture of the orchard too, without the discarded fridge, full of apple pickers standing on ladders and carrying baskets. But there were no pictures of Pebbleton House. On the next wall there were a lot of posed group photographs, adults and children wearing similar clothes to the costumes in the film, involved in various activities.

'Pebbleton Village Treasure Hunt, 1909', 'Local boy wins boat race, July 1911', 'Boatyards mourn *Titanic* sinking, April 1912', 'Soldiers recuperate at Pebbleton House, summer 1917'.

She stopped and gazed at the soldiers' faces. She had no idea what Freddie looked like, only that he had 'rough paws' for hands. That didn't help. Most of the soldiers were in uniform, buttoned and belted like Byron in the film. But several had arms in slings or patches over an eye. Two men were seated, one in a chair and the other in a wheelchair. They both wore striped pyjamas and were more heavily bandaged than the others but were smiling none the less. The soldiers were grouped together on the edge of a lawn in a formal garden, but it didn't look anything like the garden at the Pebbleton Beach Guest House. She moved closer. Was that the house behind them? Yes. Just above their heads, a little out of focus, were the distinctive roofline and crenelations, and her odd-shaped bedroom window.

Her phone buzzed.

Es, With Byron @ votre maison. In LURVE! Where R U? Mol xoxoxoxoxox

On a normal day, she would have dashed straight back to the hotel to make sure her friend didn't get too much flirting time with Byron. But it wasn't a normal day. Somehow, Esther's summer had turned itself upside down. The things she'd thought were important – her growing friendship with Byron, the film crew, the movie – no longer were. She had a mission, a quest that had taken hold of her heart and wouldn't let go. She'd been wrong. This summer wasn't about having fun with her mates on the beach or making her parents happy again or even falling in love with a movie star. It was all about the letters. The past now took priority over the present. The danger Freddie faced a hundred years ago in the war felt so much more important than the threat of Molly stealing Byron Gale from her.

She went back and peered at the treasure hunt photograph. It had been taken in the centre of the village, outside the Black Lamb pub. Fifteen or twenty children of varying ages were huddled together, some standing, others on their knees or sitting. All of them were in pirate costumes, though few looked exactly alike. There were black tricorn hats and spotty headscarves, eye patches and drawn-on curly moustaches. Some wore knee-length boots, striped tunics or long coats with giant buttons. Some

of the children had toy pistols tucked into leather belts and others grasped swords or wooden daggers. Esther scanned their faces. The picture had been taken more than a hundred years ago, but they could easily be today's village kids, she thought.

Her gaze travelled down to the caption beneath. 'Pebbleton Village Treasure Hunt, 1909. Black Lamb team: (back row, left to right) George Trickett, William Padsfield, John Sapsworth, James Swain, Henry Burfitt, (kneeling, left to right) Edmund Swain, William Sapsworth, Martha Padfield, Dorothea Dearlove, Frederick Blezzard . . .'

She gasped and scrutinised the picture again. She counted across the line of kneelers as her heart thumped.

The fourth and fifth faces were grinning. The two children were leaning together and their hands were tightly clasped. Dorothea Dearlove and Frederick Blezzard were obviously great friends. Best friends. Esther's pulse raced. She'd found them! She'd found Dotty and Freddie!

The next photograph she discovered was almost as exciting. It was a little further along the wall and was captioned, 'W S P U. Pebbleton Branch, June 1908'. It was of a group of women, clad all in white – long dresses, coats, jackets or skirts and blouses – standing together on the beach. They held a wide banner above their heads and wore striped sashes across their bodies. Although they were dressed the same, like a sort of uniform, each of them had put her outfit together in a unique way, just like the pirates. Several of the women had gorgeous hats, covered in flowers or feathers, while others wore flowers pinned on their clothes. The woman in the middle looked amazing. She wore a smart fitted pale jacket with full sleeves and a flamboyant striped bow tied around her waist. She had a large brooch at her throat and wisps of her dark wavy hair were escaping from a loose, cushion-shaped hairdo and floating dramatically in the wind. Esther recognised her straight away. It was Mrs Dearlove, the woman with the necklace. Dorothea's mum.

There was another face she knew too. She was a little

younger than before but it was definitely her, Dorothea the girl-pirate, with two plaits held in place with striped ribbons. She was wearing a frilly white pinafore, black stockings and lace-up boots. She also had a sash, and although she was standing in the shade of the banner, the words on it were easily legible. It said,

VOTES FOR WOMEN

The hair stood up on the back of Esther's neck.

'Woooo!' she yelped, then slapped her hand over her mouth and peeked over her shoulder. Her voice had echoed through the building, but the museum was still virtually empty so perhaps nobody had heard her.

They'd studied the suffragettes (and the suffragists – she always mixed up which was which) in Year Eight too. They'd done a sort of project on them, but she couldn't remember much detail about the campaign for women to get the vote. She knew someone had thrown herself in front of the King's horse on Derby Day, a sort of suffragette version of a suicide bomber, except she hadn't killed other people, just herself. Then there were the women who lobbed bricks through shop windows and chained themselves to railings. Some went to prison, where they would refuse to eat and were force-fed through rubber tubes. Esther shuddered at the thought.

She hurried back to the necklace. There was one other memory she had of that history project, a drawing she'd done, copying a 'VOTES FOR WOMEN' poster. She'd used a new set of pencils to colour the picture, the same colours that were in the necklace, green, white and purple. Charles Dearlove had given his wife a necklace in the suffragette colours. Cool!

She clutched the front of her sweatshirt and the letters rustled. Freddie and Dorothea were real. They had grown up in the village, just like she and her friends had done. If she'd been alive a century ago, they might have been her friends too. She knew them. She liked them. She had to read the rest of their story.

Her phone buzzed under her hands.

Es, B filming @ teasel wood. Invited ON SET!!!!! Get over here NOW! Mol x

On her way to the beach, she stopped outside the Black Lamb pub and paused where the treasure hunters had been snapped a hundred years before. Now that the film people had repainted the window frames and taken down the banner, it looked exactly the same as it did in the picture.

Chapter Fifteen

Reading while walking across the sand proved a challenge, especially with so many obstacles to dodge – small boys digging networks of moats and dams, dogs chasing wet tennis balls and barricades of picnic tables and surfboards. Why had she come this way? As if all that wasn't difficult enough, the breeze had picked up, so the thin stained paper of the letters fluttered in her grasp like a trapped bird.

Freddie's handwriting was no better in the fourth letter and this too was written in pencil.

. . . a bleak scene indeed. A forest reduced to shattered stumps, whole towns collapsed to rubble shoulder-high.

She arrived at the dunes and entered the maze of narrow gullies between grass-topped banks, allowing her feet to take her left and right, up and down, along familiar winding paths.

Her heart pounded as she turned the letter over and continued to read.

. . . we reached the outermost trenches at dusk, weary but alert to the new sights and sounds that greeted us . . . flares of white light on the horizon reminded me of the pulse of the lighthouse across the cove.

The beach bedlam and the roar of the surf faded as Esther ducked through a hole in the fence and stepped into the green calm of Teasel Wood.

Far off, like a dull rumour of some other war.

The hissing in her ears took longer to subside. A bead of sweat ran down her back, between her shoulder blades.

. . . everywhere there's mud so sticky that our boots are clogged and heavy with it. Though it's summer, we rarely see the sun. The sky is swathed in a black smoke that tastes of cordite.

Damp fern fronds stroked her legs. The path dipped and Esther came to a halt in the centre of a shallow bowl, a hushed oasis, surrounded on all sides by the ghost-like trunks of birch trees, their leaves whispering gently above. Which way? She swallowed.

... The maze of trenches twist and turn and one narrow, sandbag-lined channel can look much like another.

147

. . . Thoughts of you, my dearest Dot, are what keep me going. When it's cold as ice or the rain pelts down for days on end, in my head I am walking in summer fields with you. And you are not to worry. I will keep out of trouble. You are my treasure and when this war is over I'll be home to find you. We'll be together for-ever.

Molly's text hadn't mentioned where in the expanse of Teasel Wood she might be. The dense woodland stretched from the dunes car park, along the spine of the mile-long beach, and thinned out at the jetty where the ferry crossed to Silver Sands. Four paths bisected the quiet glade, four possible directions. Behind her was the heaving beach, ahead the main road: on the right was the path to the ferry and the left led back to Wipeout. She gazed unseeing through the trees, unable to decide.

She looked down at the fan of letters, now damp and crumpled in her tight fist. Her hot hands were shaking. How could words written a hundred years ago make her feel so afraid? The events the letters described were part of history, a distant memory, and yet she was terrified. But she had to know.

Dear Dorothea,
This is a hard letter to write.

It was the fifth, Freddie's last. She took a breath and read on.

I've seen my share of horror, Dotty, death and carnage, things I could not bring myself to describe to you. But today I lost a friend and the pain in my heart is worse than any shrapnel wound, worse than drowning in mud,

148

worse than losing an arm or a leg.

Will Sapsworth died right in front of me. Shot by a sniper's bullet. A blessing, I suppose, for it would have been quick. But all I can think of now is that it might have been me. If I'd chosen to lean against that wall while we waited for the light of the flares to fade, instead of crouching like a coward, as I did, I would be dead too.

An unusual tiredness flooded Esther's body and drained all the energy from her limbs. She wanted to curl up in a humid nest of soft bracken beneath a tree, press pause, breathe in the undergrowth and sleep.

She jumped at a sharp sound, like a gunshot, to her left. The stillness and solitude of the clearing was no longer comforting, the excess of green felt poisonous instead of peaceful. She set off hurriedly up the left-hand slope.

Ahead, pale shapes began to appear through the trees. The same sound echoed again, this time a little louder: a single crack, a ball against a bat or a branch against a tree trunk. A few steps further and one of the pale shapes became the side of a white truck, another a cluster of sail-like hooded spotlights and giant silver reflectors.

'Hey, this is private property.' A man wearing a rustling black cagoule stepped out from behind a tree and blocked her path. 'This area is out of bounds,' he barked. A strap around his neck held a plastic card proclaiming 'LAST POST FILMS – SECURITY' in aggressive red capitals.

Esther froze. Nobody had ever stopped her in Teasel Wood before. She'd hung out with friends and built dens here, year round, since she'd moved to Pebbleton, and her friends assured her that generations of kids had been doing so for ever. Despite the very old, broken-down fence, they'd never thought that the wood might actually belong to someone.

'Oh . . . um . . . s-sorry,' she stuttered. 'I-I didn't...'

'It's OK, Kevin, she's with me.' Molly trotted towards them, leaping over the ferns like a nervous deer. 'This is my mate, Esther. Can she sit with me? I promise she'll keep out of the way too.'

'Awight,' Kevin mumbled.

'Thanks,' Esther said to Kevin. How did Molly know he was called Kevin? Before she could ask, Molly had grabbed her arm.

'What took you?' she said.

Esther shook her head. She didn't know how to explain why she'd gone the long way around, or that she'd walked really slowly so she could read. She didn't know where to start.

'What's that?' Molly asked.

Esther was still clutching the letters, a paper posy in each hand. 'Nothing.' She shoved them into her pocket. 'Tell you later.' She faked a smile. 'Where's you-know-who?'

'Rehearsing. Come on. It's a really brilliant scene, *très* clever.' She began to wade backwards through the fronds. 'Tom, you know, Byron's character, has been, like, injured and he's lying in this water-filled bomb crater, dying. And he's sort of delirious and starts imagining he's in this beautiful forest, with flowers and butterflies and stuff. They're going to do CGI and morph from the crater they've already filmed in a studio in London to Teasel Wood.' Molly stopped and grinned with pride, as if she had written the scene herself.

Esther looked up at Kevin, who shrugged and waved her on. 'Be my guest.'

She followed Molly into a clearing that was littered with metal trunks and electrical equipment. There was the usual awning over a huddle of folding chairs, occupied by the busy crew. It was a small unit, just eight or ten people, and in the centre of the activity, wearing his army uniform, was Byron Gale. He smiled and waved, and Esther smiled back, her insides performing the inevitable meltdown. She was relieved there were no flights of stairs in Teasel Wood. None the less, she took extra care not to trip over any lurking tree roots or branches as she made her way towards an empty folding chair beside Molly.

How had Molly got herself invited to the filming in Teasel Wood? How did she know so much about the scene Byron was filming? She must have come looking for Esther at the guest house but found Byron instead. A jealous nausea flipped Esther's stomach. She thrust her hands deep into her pockets, clasped her fingers over the envelopes and waited.

trenches
at dusk . . .

Lights were adjusted, make-up reapplied, hair teased and the filming began. Instead of distracting her from the letters, however, the scene had the opposite effect. Under her hands, Freddie's words burned through the paper . . .

the pulse of
the lighthouse . . .

a bleak scene indeed . . .

reduced to shattered
stumps . . .

rubble shoulder-high . . .

tastes of cordite . . .

She watched Byron pretending to die of his wounds in the Teasel Wood ferns. Over and over, take after take, punctuated by the gunshot crack of the clapper board, he gasped his lines, leaned back in the evil fronds and closed his eyes. The weight of the letters pressed down on her belly, tied knots in her bones and squeezed out her lungs.

You'd think me quite changed, not the shy boy you once knew.

The boy Dorothea once knew was a real boy, not an actor pretending.

I've seen my share of horror, Dotty, death and carnage, things I could not bring myself to describe to you.

A hundred years ago, the real boy, Freddie Blezzard, was in the trenches in France facing death at any moment. He wasn't having make-up dabbed on his nose. Freddie's uniform wasn't from a costume van. He couldn't die fifty times, then get up and go back to an elegant hotel room for a hot bath.

If I'd chosen to lean against that wall while we waited for the light of the flares to fade, instead of crouching like a coward, as I did, I would be dead too.

If Freddie had died, he'd stay dead. That was why Dorothea didn't send the last letter. Freddie was dead!

Byron tilted his chin and again a grimace corrupted his handsome features.

Poor Freddie.

Esther shook her head. The envelopes were white-hot metal against her flesh. They'd punched a hole right through her like a screaming artillery shell.

Her brain ached. Her heart screamed. Her limbs were coiled with wire, prickling with painful barbs.

Like twitching agonies of men among its brambles . . .

She couldn't breathe.

She couldn't think.

He mustn't die. He mustn't! What about Dorothea?

Byron closed his eyes again and released a final sigh.

Esther leapt out of the chair.

'Noooooo! Freddie!'
Byron's eyes flashed open.
Everything stopped.
Everyone turned.

Esther felt the blood drain from her body and feared she might faint. Molly reached out and took her arm.

'Es? You OK?' she whispered.

Esther blinked. 'What?'

'Sit down. You're supposed to be quiet when they're filming.'

'Oh. Sorry. I didn't ... Sorry.'

Esther slumped back into the chair to comply with Molly's request, but mostly because her legs were about to fold. She wasn't sure what had happened, why she'd jumped up. She rubbed her face.

Molly leaned over and wrapped an arm around her shoulder. 'Who's Freddie?' she whispered.

Esther groaned. She'd said Freddie's name out loud, made an idiot of herself again. 'He's . . . um . . . nobody. I don't know.' She looked up and peered through the curtain of hair she'd allowed to fall across her face. They were still watching her. Byron too. Another humiliation. She blew out her cheeks and hunched down into the seat. Then everyone turned away in unison. They'd heard another sound.

There were muffled voices approaching, and the confident swish of numerous feet through the undergrowth. Someone else had discovered that there was a film crew in Teasel Wood. A group of kids had sneaked in from the beach and Kevin was already crashing through the trees to head them off. A whoop went up and the kids scattered, but Esther noticed three older boys, who skirted around and appeared again at the other side of the clearing. There was something strangely familiar about one of them, something that sent a warm thrill up her spine.

'Are you sure you're OK?' Molly asked.

Esther flinched. Molly was frowning at her.

'Fine.' Esther tried to fake a smile. She looked back at the trio and found the face again. Her heart leapt in her chest. The tallest boy was wearing shades and a surfer's hat. Max had a hat just like it. The boy turned his head. Not only did it look exactly like Max's hat, the boy looked exactly like Max. It *was* Max!

Chapter Sixteen

By the time she got to the hole in the fence, the kids and the three older boys had dispersed across the dunes. Which way had Max gone? she wondered. She'd taken too long to get out of the clearing, giving Molly a stupid, obviously made-up excuse for her sudden exit. She cringed at her clumsiness, the embarrassing spectacle she'd made of herself, and then at the realisation that she'd left Molly alone with Byron again.

But she couldn't worry about that any more. Max was home. Her brother was home. If Max was back, it meant she could cope with anything. She could put up with Molly's blatant flirting, the invasion of the guest house, Dorothea's unopened letter and even the hideous wallpaper scar in her bedroom. If Max was home, everything would be great again.

She jogged down the central path through the dunes. Maybe she would catch up with him on the beach.

'Hey, Esther!'

She slowed down to a walk and looked up. Sprawled above her on a grassy ledge were five boy-shaped silhouettes. Esther raised her hand to shield her eyes, but she couldn't tell who'd spoken. 'What?' she asked impatiently, halting at the base of the bank.

'You gonna be at Wipeout tonight?' asked the voice.

Esther jiggled nervously from foot to foot and squinted. She didn't have time for these questions. The talking shape moved, casting a shadow over her, and Esther noticed that one of the silhouettes had something on his arm. A sling. It was the bruised boy.

'Um, yeah. I guess I will.' She stopped jiggling and smiled.

'I-it's my birthday,' said the bruised boy.

'Yeah? Cool.'

'You . . . um, you should come along. I'm having a sort of party. There's gonna be a band and free beer and stuff. It'll be cheesy.'

Esther nodded. 'OK. Thanks.'

She waved and grinned as she jogged away. Inside she was hugging herself. Max was home and she was going to a cool party. She couldn't wait to tell Molly that the college boys knew her name. She'd be so jealous. No, perhaps she wouldn't tell Molly. Tonight might be her last chance to impress Byron. She'd catch him before he went back to his hotel. She'd ask him to come to the party with her, tell him it was going to be the event of the summer or something, and not just some lame kid party with soft drinks and stuff. She'd totally surprise all those college

students by turning up with the movie star. It would be brilliant. And she'd stand a much better chance with him if her best friend was out of the picture. She'd just sort of forget to mention it to her. She sprinted faster. She had to catch up with Max.

The sands were teeming with people. Every inch seemed occupied, from the dunes to the water's edge. She snaked between blankets and skidding beach balls, jumped over sand sculptures and picked her way towards the beach huts. The dunes near the huts were taller than elsewhere on the beach. If she stood on the highest bank, she might spot her brother's hat again.

She dug her toes into the sand and reached up to grab tufts

of the rough grass. With each step up the slope she sank back a little, the bank crumbling underneath her shoes. But the grass roots were well anchored and she was able to use all the strength in her arms to grapple over the ledge then swing her legs up. She kneeled on the top, breathing deeply, and staggered to her feet.

Below her was a jumble of parasols and towels where countless bodies sprawled in the shade or cooked in the midday July heat. There were plenty of hats – baseball, straw, floppy brimmed, rubber swimming – but none was Max's. She looked left, followed the rippling sea of heads until they were no more than coloured dots in the far distance, then right, towards the cliff. There! There he was again!

She dropped off the edge, waded down the steep slope and landed on her knees. She pitched forward and rolled over the corner of a blanket.

'Hey!'

She looked up at a woman and two small children selecting sandwiches from a blue plastic box. Esther had accidentally flipped sand over their lunch.

'Sorry.' She climbed to her feet and backed off into the crowd.

The water's edge was less crowded but there were still lots of splashing kids to dodge. She jogged again, the wet sand sucking at her feet. Her leg muscles were burning by the time she reached the border between sand and pebbles near the cliffs. Could Max have been heading for the boathouse? She picked her way over the stones, climbed the ramp and stopped. Dad was leaning on one of the boathouse doors, pushing it closed.

'Is . . . he . . . here?' she panted, dashing past him.

'I'm closing up,' said Dad.

Max wasn't in the workshop. Maybe he was in the roof space. She made for the ladder. He had sometimes slept in the boathouse when the B&B was full. She scrambled up and peered into the dark. There was nobody upstairs either, and no sign of her brother's clothes or bags. She jumped back down, disappointed.

'Who you looking for?' Dad asked from the doorway.

'Max.' She ran out past him. 'He must be at Wipeout. Or he's gone home.'

In the guest-house lobby, sweating and worn out, she'd bumped into the two Stone Harbour girls that Mum had hired as chambermaids. They were hopeless chambermaids and Esther suspected they'd only applied for the job to get access to celebrities. Confirming her theory, instead of doing the job they were supposed to be doing - replacing towels or emptying bins upstairs - the girls were sitting together on the steps. They were mooning over the actor who was playing Tom's evil uncle.

'Did a tall boy wearing a knitted hat come through here just now?' Esther asked the girls.

'A boy?' asked one.

'Nah! No boys,' said the other.

'Didn't see no knitted hats. Just a hotty in a uniform.' They giggled stupidly and nodded at the actor in military uniform across the lobby. He was adjusting the cuffs of his braid-encrusted khaki jacket. The gold swirls resembled the scrambled egg Esther had arranged on slices of toast that morning at breakfast. He looked ridiculous. She squeezed between the two gigglers and bounded up the stairs. The chambermaids were obviously idiots. How could anyone fancy a man with such an enormous ugly moustache. They probably hadn't even noticed Max going past them. She slammed through the 'PRIVATE' door and ran straight into his room.

He wasn't there either. She took out her phone.

Max, where R U? Egg x

She dashed into her own room, closed the door and grabbed the remote for her music player. She sat on the bed, selected Max's summer playlist again and a pumping drumbeat bounced between the walls and filled the room. She opened her laptop.

Dear Max,
I saw you at Teasel Wood and on the beach. It was really mean of you to run off like that. Where did you go? I looked EVERYWHERE. Are you staying with a friend in the village? I'll understand if you don't want to come home. It is a bit mad here. But I really need to see you!

'Esther?'

Mum was outside the door.

'Go away!' Esther had not forgiven her for the wallpaper.

'Are you OK, sweetheart?'

She didn't want Mum to come in, so she leapt to her feet, picked up her desk chair, tilted it and rammed the back under the door handle like she'd seen people do in movies. It worked. The door was wedged shut and when Mum turned the doorknob and tried to open it the chair jerked but held fast.

'Go away,' Esther repeated. 'I don't want to talk to you.' She pressed the remote's volume button and the band played louder.

'Molly's here,' said Mum behind the door. 'She's worried about you. Says you ran off in a bit of a state just now.'

'Tell her to go away,' Esther shouted. 'I'm not talking to her either.'

She was furious. Not only had Molly tried to steal Byron away from her, she'd come running over to the guest house and grassed about what happened in Teasel Wood. Friends shouldn't do stuff like that. True friends didn't flirt with boys you fancied, and they always kept your secrets, no matter what they were. She wasn't going to tell Molly about the letters. Not now. And she definitely wouldn't tell her about the party. No way.

There was a muffled conversation out in the hallway. Was that Dad's voice too? She could have turned the music down to be sure, but she didn't want them to think she cared what was going on outside.

'Esther?' said Mum, softly, then a little louder, 'Esther. Dad's concerned about you as well. Can he come in?'

'No! Go away, all of you!'

'Something's up, Omelette,' said Dad's voice. 'What is it?'

'I'm fine. Everything is fine. Just leave me alone.'

'Molly says you were upset. What upset you, Es?'

'It's none of her business and it's none of yours,' she spat, then immediately regretted it. She wasn't angry with Dad. It was Mum and Molly she hated. But all three of them were outside the door, and if she opened it to Dad, the others would probably barge in. Was there nowhere she could find any privacy any more? What had happened to respecting personal space? The only one she really wanted to speak to was Max.

There was more muttering outside and the doorknob jiggled. Then silence. Esther calmed herself by tapping her foot in time to the second track, something indie from the nineties.

'Um, Esther.' Dad's voice wobbled. 'You come out when you're ready. We're all going to go downstairs. I'll make you a cup of tea. All right?' He was talking like Esther was a three year old.

'All right,' she answered. She tapped her foot harder and jiggled her knee up and down. The wallpaper scar leered down at her.

Max, I can't bear this summer without you here! Mum has violated my personal space, Dad is treating me like a baby, my best friend is a traitor and my room has been destroyed! All I need now is for Gull to set fire to my surfboard and I'll have the full teen-angst box set!

Please, please, please come home!

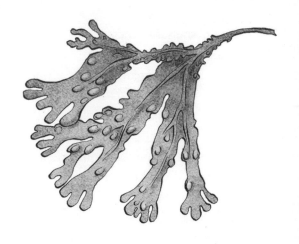

Chapter Seventeen

Nobody noticed her sneaking out through the garden. She walked along the sand, heading northwards, looking for a quiet spot. A place to think. The shoreline was still busy. Near the beach huts a cluster of younger girls were dragging sticks and pieces of driftwood across the flat wet sand, tracing a pattern into the smooth surface. They had collected little piles of white pebbles from the other end of the beach, below the cliff, and now began to arrange them, side by side, along the lines they'd drawn. They were decorating the edges of their elaborate carpet with small shells and knots of dark, leathery seaweed.

'What ya doing?' Esther asked. They were Gull's age but she didn't recognise them. A girl with bare feet and rolled-up jeans looked up.

'Writing,' she said, and smiled.

'Writing what?'

'It's—' the girl began, but her blond friend stopped her, taking hold of her arm. 'Don't tell her.'

'I'm not,' the barefoot girl asserted, and looked back at Esther. 'It's a secret.'

'It's a message,' said the blond friend proudly.

'You said don't tell her,' said the barefoot girl, annoyed.

The girls jostled each other, then returned to their task.

'What sort of message?' Esther asked.

The girls ignored her.

Esther looked down at the pattern then twisted her neck left and right, trying to decipher it.

'Can't read it,' she said. 'Not much of a message if you can't read it.' She snorted.

Barefoot girl stopped again, put her hands on her hips and glowered at her. 'We've only just started. And anyway, it's a *secret* message. It's supposed to be so you can only read it if you go up there.' She pointed to the top of the cliff.

'Cool!'

The blond girl slapped her friend's thigh with her stick. 'Popp-eeee! It's not a secret any more if you tell everyone.'

'Ow!' Poppy squealed. 'She's not everyone, stupid. It's Max's sister.'

'Oh.' The blond girl tugged nervously at her T-shirt and walked away.

Esther walked on, deep in thought and unaware of where her feet were taking her. She kept walking until she reached the furthest tip of the shore at the ferry terminal. There she climbed up on the metal barrier by the jetty and hooked her ankles behind the horizontal crossbar. The metal was cold against her flesh and made her ankle bones ache. She watched the cars and holidaymakers climbing off and on the ramp for a while. People were still streaming back and forth to Silver Sands. Then she turned round and started back. There was nowhere quiet at this end. She'd try south.

Bright red stars danced on the inside of her eyelids. The evening air was humid and heavy inside the boat, where the sea breeze couldn't reach her. She felt safe in her warm cocoon, even though this boat was no longer seaworthy and had lain wrecked and abandoned for years at the unpopular, pebbly end of the beach. The puckered, sun-bleached wood prickled against her back as she swapped legs and rested her other foot over the side. She wondered why she'd never thought to hide in the boat before. It was perfect. At last she'd found some personal space.

The reclaiming of the sands had begun. While she'd been lying there, the sounds coming from the beach had altered. She could no longer hear the screams of children splashing in the waves, nor the chatter of their parents. They were retreating, returning to the car park, heading home.

. . . dream of golden afternoons . . . stolen beach kisses.

Esther had now read and reread the letters so many times she knew them by heart. She recited them in her head and imagined Freddie's voice.

It is an odd routine. We
sleep during the day and spend the nights
carrying rations and ammunition boxes up to the reserve
trenches. It is hard, heavy work, bent double for hours.
Soon I shall resemble that bag-of-bones carthorse
ploughing my uncle's fields.

175

. . . Tonight it was sardines on toast. I would give all my pay for a fresh caught Smuggler's Rock mackerel with creamed horseradish.

. . . I have learned to prefer the icy cold. When the frost melts the lice begin to bite.

. . . The maze of trenches twist and turn and one narrow, sandbag-lined channel can look much like another. Sometimes a wall that existed one night has a new hole blasted through it the next. Alternatively, a new or deeper trench might have been dug or steps built where there were none. If it weren't for the mud, the rats and the snipers, I could imagine myself wandering through the dunes. . . . your picture, which lies in my breast pocket pressed against my heart.

She opened one eye and peered at the screensaver on her phone. She'd replaced the picture of her and Molly hugging each other on the last day of term with a photo she'd taken in the museum. It was a little blurred and dark, but the two happy faces smiled at her from the centre of the screen, Dorothea and Freddie. Besties. Only the picture's lack of colour made it different from all the other saved images, the people and events in her own life, captured and cherished in her phone's digital files. Now these two meant almost as much to her as Molly and Max. She scrolled though and found her favourite picture of Max, taken last summer when he was celebrating the end of his A level exams. He looked so happy raising a beer bottle, grinning at her in the summer sunshine.

There was still no message from him, but at least she now had a plan. It was a great plan, a plan that would sort everything, make everything right again. As soon as they finished shooting in Teasel Wood – when the light began to fade – she'd go and find Byron. She would prove that she wasn't insane (she didn't quite know how yet, but she'd think of something) and explain to him that Molly was a flirt, a disloyal friend and therefore not famous-actor-girlfriend material. She'd invite him to the party at Wipeout and he'd say yes, and she'd get dressed up in something really pretty, a dress maybe, and her purple suede heels. She'd be the most envied girl at the party. Then tomorrow, she would start the hunt for the Blezzards. If Max was here, he'd know where to look. She was going to find Freddie's family, and even if they lived in London or Scotland, she would deliver Dorothea's letter to them. She smiled, squeezed her eyes shut and watched the red stars dancing again.

. . . flares of white light on the horizon reminded me of the pulse of the lighthouse . . .

Poor Freddie, Esther thought. He must have been missing home. She counted on her fingers from 1909, when the treasure hunt picture was taken, until 1915, when Freddie sent the first letter. Six years. In the picture, he looked about Gull's age, thirteen or fourteen, which would make him only nineteen or twenty when he went to war, the same age as Max (he'd be twenty in January) and only just old enough to enlist.

If it weren't for the mud, the rats and the snipers, I could imagine myself wandering through the dunes.

Esther shivered as a cloud drifted over of the sun. The sticky air inside the boat stirred and spiralled. A sultry wind was churning around Smuggler's Rock and the waves made a new sound, no longer a whisper against the pebbles but an urgent clatter. Esther gazed upward. The sky beyond the cliff was smudged with charcoal. Would there be rain tonight?

The wind growled. No, it wasn't the wind. It was a voice.

'… This place is nowhere-ville, the sweaty armpit of the planet,' it said.

Heavy feet were crackling down the beach a few metres from the boat. The low-pitched voice sounded familiar. At first, Esther thought it might be Max. She was about to sit up.

'It's dead here. I'm itchin' to get back to civilisation in London.'

It wasn't Max. She slowly retracted her dangling foot and held her breath. The voice was husky and gave her chills.

Ah, Porphyro! Thy voice was at sweet tremble in mine ear . . .

'There's zero nightlife, even the clubs in Silver Sands are, like, full of Neanderthal knuckle-draggers and, don't worry, the girls here are putrid!'

It was Byron. He must have been seeking privacy too. He'd discovered this refuge at the stony end of the beach and assumed he was alone. He didn't realise she was there, hidden inside the crusty old boat.

He laughed, then was silent for a moment, listening, and Esther chewed her thumbnail. She was annoyed. Why is he being so rude about the village and Silver Sands? I thought he liked it here. OK, so it isn't London, and it's probably one of the most boring places on earth, but 'sweaty armpit' and 'the girls here are putrid'? That's just offensive.

'I had this girl all over me today, invited me to this cockroach-infested beach café. I bet there's a whole crowd of them, all lip-gloss and *Hot Dog* T-shirts, waiting for me to turn up at their sad party and, like, sign my name across their arms or something. Ha ha ha! All they want is to get papped snogging a celeb. It's pathetic... Yeah, I bet they would too... No way! I don't wanna get arrested!' He laughed and crunched along the pebbles, closer to the boat.

Esther felt sick and folded her arms across her own *Hot Dog* T-shirt, as if covering the logo would make it invisible. She scowled. Was he talking about Molly? She wasn't all over him. That was so unfair. And Wipeout was not cockroach infested. It was a little shabby and fraying at the edges but it was a really cool place. And what was wrong with lip-gloss?

'Yeah, it's a hotel . . . a guest house. It's kind of somebody's

179

home too, so I've had to suck up to the family that live there, you know, keep them sweet.'

Esther's face burned with fury.

'We wrap tomorrow, getting out of here at last. Can't wait to see you. You know you're the only girl for me.'

Esther folded her arms over her head and wished she was somewhere else. Her head spun and her insides churned. She was unsure which of Byron's revelations upset her the most. He had already been invited to the party, he was leaving, he had a girlfriend and he'd been pretending to like her because he was 'sucking up' to her family. The last one. Definitely the last one.

Byron was an even better actor than she'd thought. All those times he'd joked with her, chatted over breakfast, winked at her across the lobby, he was just pretending. What a liar! He'd fooled her, made her think that there was something between them. But there wasn't. She had to tell Molly before she had her heart broken too.

Chapter Eighteen

A warm spot of water fell out of the ink-smudged sky and splashed on Esther's cheek, another into her hair. It was starting to rain, was going to rain harder, and all the make-up she'd carefully applied would be ruined if they didn't get under cover soon. She wished she'd worn a jacket. Her dress was already a limp rag.

'Why would I lie?' she panted. Molly wouldn't slow down and Esther couldn't keep up in her purple suede shoes. Her feet were wobbling and skidding about on the uneven path and she couldn't see where she was stepping in the dark. If she wasn't careful, she risked breaking an ankle. She regretted ever putting them on, especially as it had meant climbing on a chair to reach the attic space above her bedroom and searching amongst the cobwebs for the shoebox.

'I dunno,' said Molly. 'Because you liked him first and now that he likes me you're *très* jealous.'

The tiny drops became peas, then marbles, making deep wet craters, like bullet holes, in the sand.

'I did like him, but not any more,' Esther explained.

'Fine. *So quel est le problème?*'

'Him. He's the problem. I mean, his girlfriend is the problem.' Esther was out of patience. 'And he's a liar.' Molly was being so dumb. She wouldn't listen.

'Uh.' Molly huffed and walked even faster, leaving her friend behind. 'I don't believe you. If he's got a girlfriend, why did he agree to meet me at Wipeout? You're just jealous, Es, so get over it,' she called over her shoulder. 'I don't know how to help you any more. Maybe you should talk to someone before you lose it completely.'

Esther watched the pale shape of Molly's hair swinging across her back as it disappeared into the gloom. She leaned against a wooden fencepost and unbuckled her shoes. She kicked them off angrily and flexed her liberated toes in the dust. Holding her shoes by the straps, she jogged after Molly. But she didn't really want to catch her. She wasn't even sure she felt like going to the party any more. What Molly had said about losing it made her angry, but it also made her think. Maybe she *was* losing it. In Teasel Wood she had imagined that Byron was Freddie. And then there was the boy in the knitted hat. Had it really been Max, or had she imagined him too? She'd wanted it to be him so much that she'd convinced herself it was.

The rain was falling harder, forming rivulets through her hair and dripping inside her collar. She decided to keep going. Wipeout was now closer than home and she'd have to get

under cover before it really poured down.

She could hear the thump and twang of the live band before she got to the car park. They sounded quite good. Were they boys from the college? she wondered. Max had mates who were in a band, and she and Molly had been to one of their gigs in a pub in Stone Harbour last summer. Perhaps it was the same band. She hoped it was and jogged a little faster.

She saw the lights first. The low dense cloud made the vivid flashes of red, green and yellow more intense. They throbbed out from the café's roof, turning the raindrops into a pulsing kaleidoscope. As she drew closer, there were gyrating shapes in the rain too, pumping bodies, moving as if their own limbs were creating the music. Some had flipped hoods over their heads, but most of the dancers were undeterred by the cloudburst. It was fun.

It rained harder. Esther stood at the edge of the scene, getting wetter and waiting for her cue. She watched her friend climb up the steps on to the veranda. A few other revellers, their shoulders and hair soaked and glistening, were starting to do the same. The band, who were using the veranda as a stage, found themselves surrounded by dripping teenagers but kept playing. Esther finally found the courage to make her entrance but skirted around the building, heading for the other door. She still had her damp suede shoes in her hands and decided she'd look odd if she carried them about with her all evening. Her feet were too sore and dirty to put the shoes back on, so she tucked them in a space beside the door to be collected later.

It was crowded and dark inside. She nudged her way past waving elbows, swaying backs and swinging beer bottles, desperate to find a face she recognised.

'Hello.'

She looked up from the bottle she'd been dodging. Attached to it was the bruised boy. He was grinning.

'Oh, hi.' She shuffled her dirt-encrusted feet, hoping that the dark would hide the sudden flush in her cheeks.

'Noisy in here, isn't it?'

She frowned and nodded, then realised he was right. He didn't mean that the band was loud. He was talking about the clatter of the rain hitting the metal roof. It was deafening.

'D'ya want a drink?' he asked.

She nodded again.

'They're outside. Wait, I'll get you one.'

Esther didn't want to be left on her own, so she followed him out to the veranda and watched as he jumped down the steps and grabbed a bottle and a can from a giant, ice-filled trough. A moment later he was at her side again, the bottle in his good hand and the can tucked into the crook of his sling.

'Wasn't sure if you wanted Coke or a beer. Are you allowed to drink beer?'

She grabbed the bottle and shrugged casually. 'Of course I am.' She raised it towards her mouth, then noticed it still had a lid. Her hands shook as she attempted to twist it off, but her rain-soaked fingers failed to grip the fluted edge and each feeble twist cut harder into her flesh.

'Here,' said the bruised boy, discarding the can and taking the bottle. He slipped it between his knees and twisted the top, then returned it to her with a triumphant smile.

Esther tried to ignore the beetle spinning in her stomach.

'You're quite good at that one-handed thing,' she said.

'Been practising.'

She glanced left and right but couldn't see Molly. Had she discovered Byron wasn't there and gone to find him? Perhaps she was already heading for the ferry to Silver Sands, as she'd threatened to do, and would continue her search for him in the fancy bars and clubs. She'd heard the rumours that he'd been seen there a few times. Esther didn't care any more. She wasn't even going to text Molly to find out.

It rained harder. More people joined them squeezed on to the veranda and they stood motionless, shoulder to shoulder, mesmerised by the evening's entertainment. Torrents of water were falling from a black cloud-mountain that now hung dramatically over the beach. A flash of blue light cracked the sky and the partiers cheered, their voices drowned by an explosion of thunder that shook the earth. It was like watching a 3D movie.

. . .rain soaks, and clouds sag stormy.

Dawn massing in the east her melancholy army. . .

This storm was in the west, but Esther thought the line sounded appropriate. It amazed her how much of Miserable Wilf's poetry had remained stuck in her head.

The last wet dancers surrendered and ran to press themselves up against the sides of the shack, hoping to find some shelter beneath its roof. But there were no gutters and the rain cascaded down the fluted metal, spitting out arcs of water around the building, like a sort of glass cage. They dodged inside and joined the heaving crowd.

Puddles grew and spread under the deserted plastic chairs. Tiny rivers began to carve channels across the car park and under the Wipeout tables. A second crack was followed by another explosion, deeper and more terrifying than the first. The cans and bottles in the trough now floated high in the icy water, which lapped over the edges like an overfilled bath. The puddles joined together and became pools, then lakes.

The band played on, though the jostling throng made it more difficult.

It rained harder still.

Another explosion fractured the sky and the lights went out. Girls yelped. Boys groaned. The band strummed a few unamplified chords then dribbled to a halt. Darkness and the growl of the storm enveloped them, and Esther reached out for the reassuring presence of the bruised boy's sleeve. Instead of his shirt she found his good hand. His warm fingers flinched, then slipped between hers, giving her knuckles a gentle squeeze before letting go. Electricity flashed through her body and she snatched her hand away. 'Oh! Um, sorry.'

'No. I'm sorry. You all right?'

'Uh-huh.' She nodded even though she knew he couldn't

see her. Why had she pulled away? He was only trying to reassure her and she'd freaked out like his hand was something repulsive. It was just a surprise, that was all, feeling that squeeze. She was such an idiot.

The chatter had faded to a murmur, and just as her eyes were becoming accustomed to the gloom, a tiny blue light popped into life somewhere along the veranda, then another. People were switching on their phones. The shadowy outlines of the balustrade, the chairs and the roof supports reappeared, bathed in a ghostly glow. The partiers no longer chattered or whooped at each angry crack over the ocean. They just watched in anxious silence, listening to the deluge soundtrack.

The main path from the car park to the dunes was now a fast-flowing river running past the café. The rain pounded harder and a sudden wave swept through, lifting the leg of a white plastic chair and spinning it around in an eerie dance across the pond.

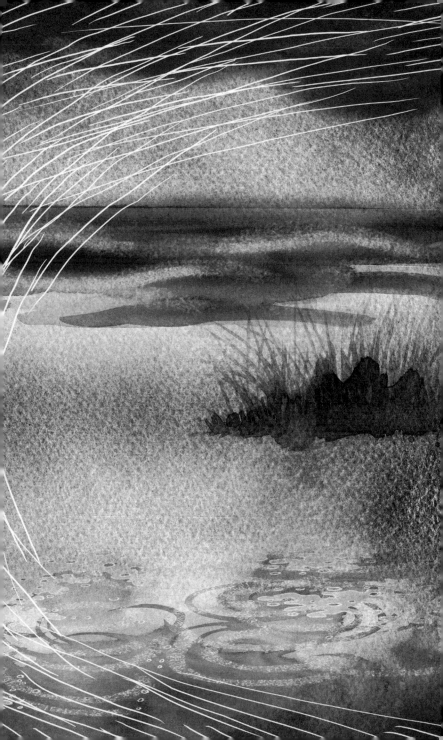

'Hey!' a boy shouted. 'Who left the taps running?'

A couple of people sniggered, nervously.

'Yeah, Finch,' said another voice. 'I think you're gonna need a plumber, dude!'

The spell broken, they all burst into therapeutic laughter.

Except for Esther, who frowned and bit her thumbnail. Her heart drummed in her chest like the rain on the roof. The words echoed inside her head, making her dizzy. *You're gonna need a plumber, dude! Gonna need a plumber. A plumber.*

'Um, I've got to . . .' She turned to the bruised boy and thrust her beer bottle into his good hand. It chimed against his own bottle and he struggled to hold on to both. His blue face crumpled in confusion.

'Sorry, I've . . . got to go.' She pushed her way out, stumbled to the steps, hesitated, curling her naked toes over the edge, then splashed down into the river. It was ankle deep. She waded out into the water and disappeared into the storm before anyone could stop her.

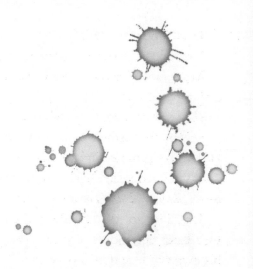

Chapter Nineteen

Yes, there it was, in the newsagent's window. She did a barefoot happy dance in the brown water that was gushing from the base of a nearby downpipe. Behind her the main street through the village was a growling torrent. But she didn't care that she was soaked to the skin and her knees and feet were scraped and bleeding. It had been worth the scramble up the mudslide path and the equally perilous ascent into the flooded village.

Since the filming of the parade had been completed, the shops had reverted to their original state and the cards and flyers had been returned to the inside of the newsagent's window. They weren't quite in the same position as before, but she'd easily found the card she'd been looking for, lower down on the right.

J C Blezzard
Friendly Local Plumber
Competitive rates No job too small

There were two phone numbers, mobile and landline, and an address – 9 Cove Road. Had she actually found Freddie's family?

Number 9 Cove Road was a Victorian villa with a red-tiled porch over the front door. It was one of ten similar houses, built at the same time, though each porch had a slight variation or a fluted ridge tile or fleur-de-lis gable, a Gothic window or cottage-style trellis. Number 9 had three elegant turned pillars, like long table legs, either side of the entrance and a narrow curved wooden beam and ring above that resembled a nose and turned-down mouth. Despite the sad face, she thought it was the prettiest.

A siren wailed and a blue light flickered on the brow of the hill and came towards her. It wasn't until it reached past the line of villas that she saw it was a fire engine. It roared and splashed a wall of water over the pavement. Esther had the sense to leap inside the porch before she was engulfed in brown sludge.

She looked out and scanned the street. It was awfully dark. Why were there no lights on in the houses? she wondered. She knew it was quite late, but were all the residents of Cove Road in bed asleep? Had the storm not woken them? The howl of the wind would have been enough to keep her awake, never mind the thunder and lightning and the machine-gun rattle of the rain on the windows. Then she noticed there were no street lights either. The power was off.

She turned to look at the front door, J. C. Blezzard's front door. How likely was it that the plumber was a relative of Freddie Blezzard? she wondered?. Pretty much a hundred per cent certain, she decided. Even if he was only distantly related, a great-uncle or third cousin twice removed, or something, he was a Blezzard and he lived in Pebbleton, so he had to be one of Freddie's descendants, didn't he? She fidgeted with excitement but couldn't bring herself to ring the doorbell, not at this time of night and not in the middle of a storm and a power cut. Anyway, she didn't have the letters with her. Or shoes. She couldn't explain about her mission to deliver Dorothea's last letter if she didn't actually have it to show to J. C. Blezzard. And he'd assume that a girl with no shoes, a soaked dress and bleeding knees must be bonkers or a stalker or something, and would probably call the police.

Just at that moment a police car whooshed by, sending another brown wave crashing over the pavement. The blue light pulsed as it disappeared into the village but there was no siren this time. Wow! she thought. This flood must be getting serious.

The Blezzards could wait until morning. She would come back with the letters in daylight, when the rain had stopped.

In the centre of the village, the water was now knee deep and fast flowing. She could hardly stay on her feet. The sound of the persistent rain crackled like bacon frying. When would it stop? Surely the clouds should be empty by now. Villagers splashed about in the street, panicking and waving torches over the water. Some even pointed upwards into the ceaseless rain, perhaps wondering, like Esther, where so much water was coming from.

The fire engine had parked at the crossroads on the edge of the torrent and the crew were knocking on doors. A fireman eased a grey-haired lady out of her cottage window and carried her to safety. Her floral dressing gown flapped around him like a scarf. Drinkers from the pub were helping the proprietor to stack sandbags in the entrance, but it was too late. The bar was already flooded. Esther watched the brown sludge churning over the pavement and wondered how deep it was at the base of Cliff Road. Might she have to swim home?

'Hey, you! Keep out of the water!' a voice yelled. She turned round. It was a policeman in a yellow jacket. 'If your house is on higher ground you should go there straight away.'

She nodded and pointed up Cliff Road. 'Up there.'

'Go around,' said the policeman. 'And stay out of the water. It's not safe.'

Esther skirted around the back of the war memorial and squelched through the churchyard to rejoin the Cliff Road above the flood. Another brown river was washing the pavement here too, but it wasn't quite as fast-flowing and she was able to splash slowly up the hill. It was exhausting, battling against the bullets of rain, the swirling wind and the muddy water dragging each footstep. The climb to her house took forever.

. . .*we cursed through sludge,*
Till on the haunting flares we turned our backs
And towards our distant rest began to trudge.
She groaned at recalling Wilfred Owen again.

The lights were out at the guest house too. An eerie sight greeted her in the driveway. Worried faces were staring from every window and dozens of eyes followed her across the soggy car park as she made her way inside. Everyone was awake and silently watching the storm. Some were in the lobby and lounge, fully dressed or in their night clothes.

A murmur echoed through the dark house, 'Esther's back, Esther's back, Esther's back.' It brought her anxious parents out into the lobby. Esther was glad they didn't make a fuss but she could tell they had been worried and were relieved she'd got home safely.

She shook water from her hair like a wet dog and stood in her rag dress at the bottom of the stairs. She realised that the thin fabric was stuck fast to her skin, revealing the outline of her underwear and the shapes of her key and phone in the skirt pocket. She pulled self-consciously at the sodden fabric around her waist. It sucked and belched against her belly. The phone beeped and she peeled the pocket open.

Es, where RU? Can't wait any longer, walking home on my own. Your fault if I drown. Mol

Esther's guts tied themselves into a guilty knot. Molly was still at the café! She'd abandoned her friend without explanation. She felt terrible and tapped at her phone with agitated wet fingers.

Mol, REALLY sorry! Thought you'd gone too. Will come and find you. Es xxx

She retreated across the lobby, but before she reached the door, Molly had replied.

Don't bother almost home. Police in my street. Night.

Esther felt her way upstairs to her bedroom and peeled off her dress in the dark. She stood in her bra and knickers, shivering for a moment, then dragged the duvet off her bed and wrapped it around herself. She went to the window and watched the cloud-reflected blue lights pulsing over the village. Her feet grew cold, so she climbed on to her bed and leaned back against the wall. A moth fluttered against the window, frantic to get out. You won't like it outside, Esther thought. It's Armageddon out there. The moth was casting a giant eerie shadow against the torn wallpaper opposite, and so was the rain running down the window. It looked like the ugly gaping wound was bleeding. Esther turned away, closed her eyes and drifted into sleep.

Flares burst in the night sky, casting a deep shadow over the pallid dunes. She walked on, her feet sinking deeper and deeper into the sand until her legs burned. At last, at a quiet crossroads, she halted. Which way? There were three deep sandy paths through the dunes. At the entrance to the left path stood a skeletal figure in a rustling black cagoule, his bloodless features half covered by a sinister hood. The right path was guarded by a child who was sitting cross-legged on a tartan rug and prising open a plastic sandwich box with a stubby flick-knife.

'Cheesy!' said the boy.

Ahead was darkness – thick, terrifying darkness – but she knew she had no choice. She had to go straight on.

A few steps into the dark trench she saw that the dunes were now lined with sandbags, wet sandbags that oozed foul water. Her feet splashed through it. She looked down. The purple suede shoes were ruined. She staggered forward and a few steps further came to the wall. Her bedroom wall. She stopped. The wallpaper was wet now. It would be easier to tear it off. She dug her nails into the paper and clawed at the edge. It came away in soggy clumps and fell into the mud at her feet. Another pair of hands appeared beside hers and she glanced over to see who had joined her in her task.

It was Max.

She smiled, and Max smiled back.

'Thanks.'

'You're going to need a plumber, dude,' he said.

Then he turned his head and she saw the jagged, bloody bullet hole in his temple . . .

Esther kicked at the duvet and wrestled herself out of the tight bundle. She was sweating and her heart pounded. She gasped for breath.

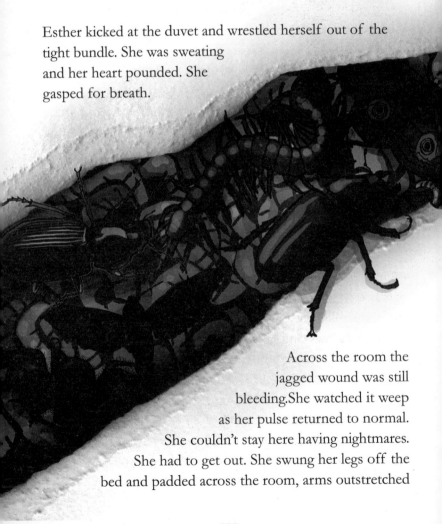

Across the room the jagged wound was still bleeding.She watched it weep as her pulse returned to normal. She couldn't stay here having nightmares. She had to get out. She swung her legs off the bed and padded across the room, arms outstretched for the doors of her wardrobe. Inside, she found her sweatshirt. She put it on and began a fingertip search for her jeans, a pair of socks and the letters. Downstairs in the laundry corridor, she pulled on an oversized raincoat and a pair of wellington boots. She stuffed the letters in a pocket, hoisted the fleece-lined hood and silently exited by the back door.

The return journey through the village was no easier. Though it was downhill, the wellingtons she'd chosen were too big and she flopped awkwardly along Cliff Road and stumbled through the muddy graveyard. She kept to the shadows and avoided any clusters of blue lights or fluorescent jackets. She didn't want to be urged to go home again. Number 9 Cove Road was still in darkness. She nipped into the porch, crouched down in a corner, drew her knees up inside the coat and closed her eyes. She would wait there till morning. There was no moth crashing against a window and no scary torn wallpaper here. This place wouldn't give her nightmares.

Chapter Twenty

'Hey! Wake up!'

Esther jerked awake. She raised her head and peered out from beneath the hood.

'You can't sleep...' The boy crouched down. 'Hey, it's you.'

She looked up. What was the bruised boy doing in her bedroom? She flexed her cold fingers. Her room was icy. Had she left the window open? At least it was too cold for the lice to bite. She smirked. Wait. Lice? Weird! She wasn't in the trenches, but it didn't look much like her bedroom either. And her duvet didn't feel right.

'What?' she croaked.

'Hello,' he said.

'What you doing here?' she asked, hoping his answer might reveal where 'here' was.

'I live here. Was about to ask you the same thing.'

Esther screwed up her face and rubbed her palm back and forth across her cold nose. It wasn't quite morning, but a liquid pre-dawn light was seeping through the gloom. It was too early to be woken. Her brain wasn't functioning.

'Where is here?' she said.

'This is my house. I mean, where I live. Thought you were a homeless person or something.'

She could still hear the hiss of rain hitting the roof and the road outside, but the wind no longer howled. The storm was dying.

'Your house?' She tried to remember what had happened last night, then recalled the porch with the sad face. 'Number nine,' she said.

'You don't look so good,' he said. 'Better come in.'

She nodded and uncurled her aching legs. She did feel quite ill, a bit queasy. Shivery, too. Her boots flapped and made a fart noise. She cringed. Why had she come here? It had seemed a sensible thing to do last night. Now she felt like an idiot.

The bruised boy put a key in the lock and opened the front door. He really did live there. She followed him inside.

'Tea?' he whispered.

She nodded. Was he being quiet because there was someone else in the house, upstairs, asleep perhaps?

He led her down a hallway to a pretty blue kitchen at the back of the house. It smelled newly painted. The boy pointed to a stool tucked under a wooden counter. She pulled it out and climbed clumsily on to the seat. She hated stools. She'd always hoped that one day she'd grow tall enough to be able to reach the seat without effort, but she still hadn't. She leaned her elbows on the counter and rested her chin on her hands. She rubbed her eyes, then watched the boy as he found mugs and tea bags, flipped the switch on the kettle and opened a pizza box that had been left on the side. He picked up a limp, gory wedge and waved it at her. She shook her head and scrunched her eyes closed, feeling quite sick again.

The kettle roared then clicked off. He poured water into the mugs, then opened the fridge and pulled out a carton of milk. He sniffed it, then carried it and the mugs over to Esther. A cloud of steam rose and swayed between them. Neither of them could think what to say next, so they remained awkwardly silent.

At last, the boy coughed. 'Why d'you run off . . . last night? Did I . . . y'know, I mean, I'm sorry about . . . your hand . . . ' He looked down into his mug.

'No! No, it wasn't that. I just remembered something, that's all.'

'Right. I thought I'd freaked you out or something.'

'No.' She shook her head and closed her eyes, recalling the warmth of his hand and the exciting jolt of electricity she'd felt when he'd squeezed her knuckles.

'Your friend looked for you everywhere.'

Esther's stomach flipped at the memory of Molly's text. 'I know.'

He poured milk on top of his tea bag and the two liquids swirled.

'What did you remember?'

She looked up. 'A card I'd seen.'

'Oh.' He looked perplexed.

She wasn't explaining herself very well. She'd have to think of a better way to bring up the subject of Freddie's letters. She raised her hand and began to chew her thumb.

'Wipeout is wrecked.' He shook his head. 'The wind just tore it apart. The beach is a mess too.'

'Did you only just get back, then?' she asked.

'Uh-huh. We all took refuge in the church hall with Finch. Came home to change so I can go back and help clean up.'

Esther replayed the events of the previous evening and shuffled them in her mind, putting them in the right order. She'd left her shoes at the café. A mountain of black cloud had hung over the beach. The sky had cracked with terrifying thunder and lightning. The world had flooded and she'd run off into the darkness.

'You're gonna need a plumber, dude,' she mumbled.

'What?'

'Nothing . . . I mean, isn't this the plumber's house? It's nine Cove Road, right?'

'Uh-huh.' He frowned.

'That's why I left the party last night.'

'To find a plumber?'

'No. I found these letters and I've been looking for someone called Blezzard and then I remembered a card in a window, a plumber called J. C. Blezzard, who lives here.'

209

'Not any more,' said the boy.

'Oh.'

He hoisted the tea bag out of his mug and dumped it on the counter. It oozed like the sandbags in Esther's dream.

'Died back in January.' The boy looked sad.

Esther sagged inside the coat. J. C. Blezzard was dead. What would she do now? She wanted to cry.

'Me and my dad are sorting through his things, doing up Grandad's house before we sell it.'

'You and your dad?'

'Yeah. I live with my mum since they split, but just for the summer, I came to help Dad.'

'Oh, that must be . . . hard.' She didn't know quite what to say.

'We used to live in the village when I was a kid, so it's been kinda cool catching up with my old mates.'

She felt sorry for him but didn't know how to tell him without sounding stupid. His arm was in a sling, his party had been ruined, his parents were divorced and his grandad was dead. Her heart pounded in her chest like an artillery barrage.

'J. C. Blezzard was your grandad?'

'Yeah.'

Esther sat up. 'So that would make you a Blezzard too, right?' A buzzing sound filled her ears. Her head was spinning.

'Yeah. Freddie Blezzard. That's me.'

He grinned at her, but Esther was already half-way off the stool. She staggered backwards and the stool tipped to the floor with a hollow clatter.

'Freddie? Y-you're Freddie?'

He nodded. He was startled.

'No. You can't be. Freddie's in France. He never came back.'

'Not me.' He frowned.

Feeling dizzy, Esther leaned against the wall. She was confused. She couldn't think. She couldn't breathe.

'You're Freddie? Freddie Blezzard?'

'Yep.'

'When, I mean, how. . ? You were in the war . . . ' She trailed off uncertainly.

'This?' said Freddie, raising his injured arm. 'Did it weeks ago, on my board.'

'Board? What board? Were there boards in the trenches?'

Freddie shook his head. His brow was pleated with confusion.

'They'll send you back when you're better, won't they?' she sobbed, and yanked the letters out of her pocket. She watched their fragile pages flutter on to the counter, distorted through the prism of tears. She put the unopened one on the top. 'You'd better have these, your letters. The top one is from Dorothea. I think she never sent it because she thought you were dead.' She sniffed and wiped her dripping nose with the back of her hand. 'That's why I came looking for you, Freddie, so I could deliver Dorothea's last letter.'

Freddie looked alarmed. He had no idea what she was talking about. She was a crazy person again. He picked up the letter and read the address.

'Frederick Blezzard?' It *was* his name. 'Hey, amazing!'

'That's you, right? Freddie Blezzard. The letter is for you.' She turned and lurched towards the door.

'I . . . I don't . . . wait!'

Esther kept going. She'd accomplished her task. She took hold of the latch, wrenched the front door open and stepped out into Cove Road.

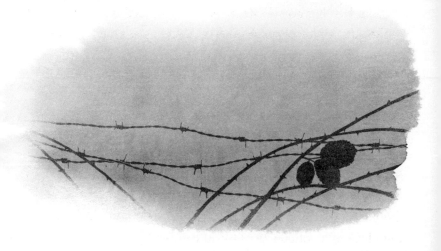

Chapter Twenty-One

'DANGER – BEACH CLOSED' said a metal sign at the head of the dunes footpath. 'By order of Greymouth Police.' Blue and white plastic tape had been stretched between the fence and the 'TO THE BEACH' signpost. Its short tail fluttered frantically in the wind. Steam was rising along the path, marbling the air with pale, restless ghosts. Weak sunlight was doing its best to break through the mournful haze that hung over the sea.

Esther kept walking. She had no idea where she was going, just away. Away from Freddie, away from her cursed home, away from having to deal with the trauma that was her life.

The entrance to the car park was blocked too. This time there was a sentry as well, a policeman in a yellow jacket. The enemy. Perhaps he was the same officer who'd spoken to her last night. She stopped and retreated before he spotted her.

She returned to the dunes footpath. This time she ignored the 'DANGER – BEACH CLOSED' sign, dipped under the police tape and crept down the path. The rubber boots made far too much noise. They sucked and pinched at her ankles with each heavy step. If she wasn't careful, the enemy might spot her. There might be patrols on the beach or snipers crouched behind the sand dunes. Her breath was quick and short.

At the edge of the car park, she eased back her hood and blinked. Had she taken a wrong turn? Had she walked too far and found herself in a foreign car park beside some other dunes? There were three abandoned cars, and between them, last night's battle had cut long, deep gullies in the wet earth as if some giantess had left impressions of her heavy tresses. A vast hairball of fence posts and wire had been pitched across the car park and had come to rest in the mouth of the beach

path. Seagulls screamed and swooped above the scattered contents of numerous rubbish bins.

She had to get to the other side without being seen. She'd make a run for it. She looked left and right. All was still. Now! She flapped awkwardly across to the far side, a lump in her throat. She skirted the fence post hairball, threw herself over a low bank and lay in a shallow ditch, getting her breath back. She'd made it unscathed.

What was she doing? She sat up. Last night was a storm, just a storm, not a battle. There were no patrols or snipers, no enemy lurking in the dunes. This was the beach, not the trenches.

She was so confused. Freddie's letters had upset her more than she'd realised. And studying those war poets must have affected her too. She stood up and brushed the wet sand off her jeans, then continued to the edge of the Wipeout clearing.

The first thing she saw was the roof. The hotchpotch of corrugated-iron panels lay perched on a sand dune ten metres from the shack. Blown off, as if by the blast of a shell. The fierce gale had lifted it and flung it carelessly aside. She was relieved to see that the shack, despite being roofless, was intact, the caravan and veranda still connected. But it looked naked. Something was missing – Finch's collection. All his accumulated flotsam and jetsam had been washed or blown away. Even the zigzag-painted radio was gone.

As Esther took in the devastation, Finch appeared at the door of the caravan with a green plastic broom in his hand. He leaned over and swept a frothy wave of brown water out on to the sand. She was about to wave and call out when, in the corner of her eye, three heads appeared behind the detached roof. They bobbed back down, appearing again further along the sand dune. Enemy soldiers. Her heart was in her mouth. She shook her head. Not soldiers. They weren't in uniform. One of the heads was wearing a knitted hat. She watched as the three figures crawled over the top of the bank and scuttled to the edge of the veranda, where they each grabbed two beer bottles from the trough, then dashed away again. They'd been so quick she'd had no time to think, and they were already racing across the dunes when she yelled, 'Hey, thief! Hey, Max!' and gave chase.

She was furious with Max. He hadn't answered her text or come home when she'd pleaded. He kept running off when he must have known how desperate she was to see him. Now he'd stolen beer from Finch. That was looting, and it was unacceptable!

She pounded along the maze of paths, getting more and

more angry. The oversized boots were impossible, like running through porridge. She hit a clump of wet grass and it sent her sprawling forward on to her knees in the damp sand. She was winded, and crouched for a moment until her pulse slowed.

'Hey, Es!'

She looked up. The boys were slouched above her in a dry alcove cut into the side of a sandbank. They were already chugging back the beers and laughing.

'Max, you nicked those! I saw you!'

'Gull,' said Max.

'What?'

'Gull,' he said again. 'Gull-i-ver.'

Esther frowned. What did he mean? Then she covered her face with her hands. He was wearing Max's hat, Max's jacket and jeans and shoes, but he wasn't Max. He was Gulliver. He was her *younger* brother.

She turned away.

It had been Gull all along. Not Max. It had never been Max. Max hadn't come home.

She stumbled back along the path, blinded by her tears. Max wasn't Max and Freddie wasn't Freddie. What was going on? Was she crazy? Finally defeated by the boots, she pulled them off and discarded them in the rough grass. Then she ran and ran and didn't stop until she got to the cliff path.

She was close to the edge, too close. A careless gust thrown up from the beach below might catch her, tip her off balance and send her staggering forward or sideways. Her feet might find a loose patch of chalk. She might slip and be carried towards the crumbling rim.

She took a shuddering breath, tipped her head back and groaned.

'Uuuuaaahhhh!'

The spiteful wind snatched her voice away as she forced out the last dregs of air and purged her lungs. The pain was still there, a dark, suffocating poison clogging her thoughts and tying knots in her gut. She rubbed the tips of exhausted fingers across her eyelids, pressing hard into the sockets. She swallowed, tasting salt – the salt of the sea and of her tears. The breeze returned to tease her hair and whip it against her neck. A strand found its way into the corner of her mouth. She spat, then scraped it out and tugged it behind her ear. She leaned into the wind and it pushed back stubbornly against her aching limbs. She closed her eyes, sighed and swayed, surrendering.

There was someone behind her. She could feel a shape deflecting the wind and muffling sound. She could sense the heat of their body. She waited for a hand on her shoulder or slipped around the crook of her arm, dragging her to safety. She waited, fearful. Brittle. One touch and she'd lose control again. One touch and she might crumble like the chalk cliff, shatter into tiny pieces and blow away, dust on the breeze. But the touch never came. The figure simply stepped forward and stood beside her, silent, reassuring. Without moving her head, she stole a look through trembling hair.

She knew it would be him.

'Don't . . . I can't . . . please . . . I can't . . .' she whispered.

He said nothing.

She sniffed. 'I'm not . . . I wasn't going to, you know . . . if that's what you were thinking. I just . . . just came here to think.'

She stared out across the churning sea.

He said nothing.

'I'm OK,' she said.

'I miss him too,' said Gulliver, softly.

'I know.'

'We've all been dealing with it in our own way.'

She nodded.

'Some more successfully than others.' His mouth formed a crooked, wry smile. 'Mum drinks too much. Dad spends far too much time alone with his boats. I've claimed Max's wardrobe. And you . . .' He shrugged. 'You just pretend he's gone to uni.'

Esther chewed her thumbnail.

'We should talk more,' Gull went on. 'You know, share what we're feeling and not keep our worries to ourselves. It's not good doing that.'

Esther looked at her younger brother. When had he got so grown-up, so wise? Perhaps his way of grieving for Max had been the best one. Yes, he'd been angry, got into trouble, been thrown out of school, but he seemed the sanest of them all.

'Look,' said her wise brother. He pointed at the beach.

Esther held back her hair and looked down at the long wedge of sand and the labyrinth of dunes beyond. Both were strewn with wreckage from the storm, shattered fence posts, tumbling drinks bottles, balls of wire, broken packing crates and fluttering plastic bags. There were a few people there too, people who had ignored the signs and made the pilgrimage to the wounded beach. Gull was pointing at a group of girls, the ones Esther had seen writing the secret message in the sand. They had repaired it, replaced all the white pebbles that had been dislodged by the waves. Up here on the cliff path, what they'd written was easily readable.

'Oh!' She burst into tears again and thrust her face into her hands. 'It's today, isn't it?'

'Uh-huh,' said Gull. 'A year ago today.'

His sweatshirt buzzed and he drew out his phone.

'It's a text from Dad.'

Esther sniffed.

'E not in her bed,' Gull read. 'Will you search the beach?'

Esther wiped her eyes and watched her brother's thumbs clicking a message back.

E here with me. Going to our bench.

He pressed send and Dad replied seconds later.

Mum and I will meet you there. Dx

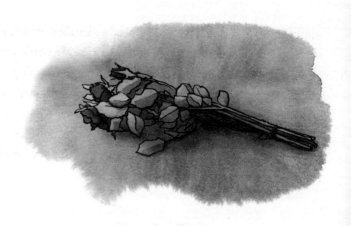

Chapter Twenty-Two

Together they walked slowly along the cliff path towards the lighthouse. Esther had never felt so tired, so disconnected. Her limbs were numb. She watched her mud-soaked socks take each step as if they clad someone else's feet. They propelled her forward, on autopilot, an unconscious bodily function like the pumping of blood through her heart or the filling and draining of her lungs. She was powerless to halt this persistent mechanism, this entity of flesh and bone, wire and fibre to which her fragile brain was attached. A brain that wasn't ready. It screamed 'go back', but her feet trudged on.

...a drowsy numbness pains
My sense as though of hemlock I had drunk...

Her senses were numb. She felt medicated, tranquillised. That emo Keats really had a handle on teen angst.

'I haven't been up here since last summer,' she said.

'I know.'

Esther's feet were taking almost two steps for each of Gull's long strides. When had he grown those legs? she thought. When had he become so like his older brother?

'I suppose I've been avoiding this place like everything else,' she said.

Gull said nothing. He didn't have to. She knew he understood.

The path climbed a small hill, and when they reached the brow she could see the remaining ribbon of chalk weaving its way to the lighthouse. She could see the bench too, just off the path, only twenty steps away, maybe fewer. Esther's feet hesitated, and this time it was Gull who propelled her on. He

drew closer and, like a dog protecting nervous sheep, urged her gently down the slope.

They arrived at the bench and sat. Gulliver leaned back, but Esther perched on the edge, her hands rammed deep into her coat pockets. She stared out across the squally sea. The sun had succeeded in burning off the morning mist and she turned her face to catch some of its heat. If she sat like this for long enough, on the hard edge of the seat, she'd get a red line across the top of her legs like she had from the bath. But she didn't want to slide backwards.

She would have to confront it eventually. But what harm was there in waiting just a little longer? Just a few minutes more soaking up the sun, enduring the discomfort of the seat.

No. She should do it now. Get it over with.

She took a deep breath, shifted sideways and twisted around. She focused on the brass plaque fastened to the top rail and read the inscription:

In memory of Maximillian Armstrong,
beloved son, devoted brother, loyal friend,
taken from us too soon.

The sun rose higher and the Armstrong family sat, arm in arm, on the bench and talked. They talked about Max, his infectious laugh, his languid walk, his stinking sports kit.

They smiled.

They cried.

They remembered.

Later, they made their way, still arm in arm, to a layby on the Stone Harbour road, where they found that a small crowd had gathered – Molly and Esther's friends from the high school, Gull's mates, and several of Max's friends back from their first year at far-flung universities. An awkward hush descended. Voices rose no louder than a whisper and heads hung in quiet contemplation. Feet shuffled and nervous eyes looked down at fingernails or the pavement. Nobody dared to look at the dry, blackened corpses of a multitude of floral tributes that had spent a year taped to a lamp post, growing more limp and desiccated as each month had passed. The friends huddled together and exchanged sombre glances.

A truck thundered by, throwing spray at their feet and ballooning their clothes, but nobody moved. Eventually, their collective torpor became too much for Molly. She wrapped her arms around her best friend and squeezed.

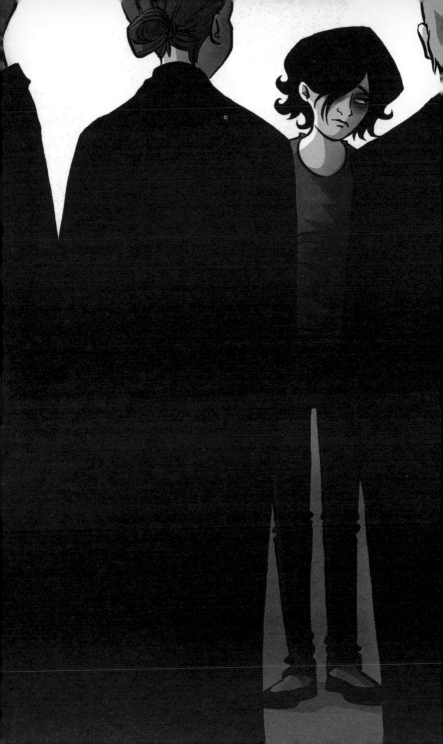

Esther's muscles remembered the same embrace a year ago. People had hugged her all day after Max's funeral. They hadn't said much, just pressed her against their bodies as if a cuddle would put her shattered life back together again. She had drifted around the guest-house garden, searching for comfort among the black suits and vegetarian canapés, overhearing hushed conversations about dangerous roads, cycling at night, a promising young life cut short. She had avoided her mum and dad. Silent and haunted, their stillness had scared her. Gulliver had scared her too, his violent agitation the complete inversion of her parents' inertia.

When Molly let her go, Esther tried to speak.

'I'm...'

'No,' said Molly. 'You don't need to mention last night. It's fine. I understand.' She tilted her head, like she did when she was flirting, and said, 'I know how *très difficile* it's been for you, Es. We're all here because we love you, all of you. Yes, even Gull.' She smiled and winked at him. 'And we thought Max was an awesome dude. A *très* awesome dude.'

The friends mumbled in agreement.

Esther smiled. 'A *très* awesome dude? Molly, you're priceless!' She sniggered and hugged her back. The friends let out a sigh and allowed smiles to break across their faces.

The angry wind that had accompanied the previous night's storm was making a final assault around Smuggler's Rock and whipping along the road. It was perfect surfing weather. There would be foam-topped waves rolling and crashing on to the beach.

'Feel that?' said one of Gull's mates. He tipped his head into the wind and closed his eyes. 'I think we should get our boards.' He waited for agreement but found only an anxious silence. 'It's what Max would want us to do,' he added with a grin.

'Yeah,' said Gull. 'He would. Get your wetsuits on, guys. We're gonna surf for my brother.'

Chapter Twenty-Three

It was miraculous that it had survived. The only feature on the beach that hadn't been battered and bruised by the storm was the old wrecked boat. Wipeout had been decapitated and stripped naked. The boathouses had lost wooden cladding and shingles from their roofs. The beach huts were now full of musty furniture with knee-deep saltwater stains. The flood had cut new gullies through the dunes and even the cliff had extra wrinkles and cracks all over her face. But the boat was intact, not a rough board out of place. It hadn't weathered the storm entirely unscathed, though. When the gale had swept the high tide right up the beach, it had lifted the old boat, and transported it five metres inland. Now it was balanced proudly on a stone plinth, where it could survey the entire mile of sand.

Esther, Gull and Molly sat inside *SS Indestructible* – the boat's new name. The surfers had begun to tire and were padding up the sand towards evening gatherings in the dunes. But Esther, her brother and her best friend had craved a little solitude. The last few days had been exhausting, emotionally draining.

There was one thing that still troubled Esther. She'd been churning it around and around in her mind since the storm. She was worried about Freddie. Both Freddies – the one who'd written the letters and the boy with the sling. She was so embarrassed about her behaviour in Cove Road. OK, so there was a sort of rational explanation for what she'd said and done – the stress of having their home invaded by a film crew, the discovery of the letters and her family coming apart at the seams had sent her a little crazy. Most disturbing of all had been the unsent letter. She'd spent far too much time fretting about it.

Of course, there were plenty of reasons why it had never been sent. She knew that now. Maybe Dotty had decided not to post it. She might have changed her mind about what she'd written. Esther did that all the time: deleting a message that might have taken an hour to write. Perhaps the letter had been propped on the mantelpiece prior to posting, had fallen behind the wall and been forgotten. Or Freddie might have come home, so Dotty had been able to tell him its contents in person.

Esther stretched her arms and gripped the sides of the *SS Indestructible*. She closed her eyes and exhaled. But she couldn't avoid considering the mostly likely reason, that Freddie had been killed in action. He had died. That was the horrible truth that had festered in the back of her mind. Dotty had written the letter, heard the devastating news, been dreadfully upset and had decided to keep it, unopened, as a memento.

And now she might never discover which of her possible solutions was the correct one. She'd thrown the letters at the bruised Freddie Blezzard then she'd run away. He would think she was a freak and would, no doubt, make every effort to avoid her until he went back home to his mum at the end of the holidays.

Footsteps crunched below her on the pebbles. She opened her eyes and looked down. At first she assumed her mind was playing tricks again. It looked like the bruised boy was standing beside the boat. She rubbed her eyes and looked again. No, it really was him. It was Freddie Blezzard, the plumber's grandson. He no longer had his arm in a sling and he was carrying a brown cardboard box. Esther's stomach beetle woke up and scuttled.

'Hi,' she said, feeling like she might throw up at any moment. She prayed that she wouldn't. That would be the ultimate humiliation.

'Hullo,' said Freddie. 'I've been looking for you everywhere.'

'Yeah?'

'You OK?'

'Uh-huh.' She was confused. Instead of avoiding her, it seemed he was doing the opposite. But there was no way that Esther wanted to talk about herself, especially if it meant having to explain what had happened in his kitchen, so she asked, 'Where's your sling?'

'Arm's all better.' Freddie lifted his elbow. 'Saw the doc this morning. Said I should start moving it.'

Esther managed a tense smile, and nodded.

'I . . . er . . . I heard about your brother. I'm really sorry. I guess you must have been...'

'Yeah. Thanks.' She was apprehensive. Where would the conversation go next? Why had he been searching for her? Was it just to offer his condolences, or was it something else?

Freddie looked down at the ground, unsure what to say.

'Um . . . why were you looking for me?' she prompted.

'Oh yeah.' Freddie shifted the box from under his good arm into both hands. 'Stuff to show you.'

'Me?'

'Uh-huh. My grandad's stuff.'

'Oh.' Esther's beetle scurried in circles.

'Shall I climb up?' Freddie asked.

'Yeah, come up,' said Molly, who had been listening to their conversation with growing curiosity.

Freddie climbed into the boat.

'Hi,' he greeted Gull and Molly.

'Yo,' said Gull, casually tilting Max's sunglasses in greeting. 'You got home all right, then?' he asked Molly. 'From the party?'

'Duh, no, I drowned,' she said. 'Stop small-talking. This isn't a vicarage tea party. Open the stupid box!'

Freddie laughed, placed the box on the floor of the boat and flipped open the lid. First he took out the letters and handed them to Esther. 'Here. I want to return these. I hope you don't mind, but I read some of them. Not the sealed one. I know you said it was for me because of my name, but it's not really, is it?'

241

'No. S'pose not.' Esther's hands trembled as she took the paper bundle.

'Then I asked my dad about Freddie, you know, the other Freddie.' He smiled. 'And he thought we might have had a relative called Frederick Blezzard who fought in the Great War and I should look in Grandad's things. I found these.'

He reached into the box, pulled out a leather-bound notebook and handed it to Esther. She turned it over, running her fingers across the textured black cover. In the bottom right corner three gold letters had been stamped, 'F.W.B.'. Esther glanced up at Freddie, her eyes wide with wonder.

'Open it,' said Freddie.

Esther eased her fingers under the cover and opened it at the first page, where she found a pencil drawing of a lighthouse, the Pebbleton lighthouse. Her stomach beetle was in a frenzy. She turned the fragile lined paper, finding pencilled notes, mundane lists and everyday jottings. But she wasn't interested in what F.W.B. had written. She was captivated by the handwriting. Those looping *l*s and swirly *e*s were instantly recognisable. They were identical to the loops and swirls in the letters. They had been written by Frederick Blezzard, Dorothea's Frederick.

'It's the same as the letters, isn't it?' said Freddie.

Esther couldn't speak. Her head was spinning.

'My dad called his Great-Aunt Flossie. She said Frederick was my great-great-grandfather.'

'Yeah?' Esther gasped. She was fighting back tears. 'W-what happened to him?' She looked at Freddie. 'I mean, did he, you know, survive the war?' As soon as the question was out of her mouth, she wished she could suck it back in. She knew what the answer would be and didn't want to hear it.

'Flossie thinks he was wounded in France in 1916 and sent home. I'm not sure how reliable her memory is, but that's the family story that's been handed down. It's what she was told, anyway.'

'Wounded?'

'Uh-huh.'

'Not killed.'

'Don't think so.'

Esther swallowed. They must be wrong, she thought. Great-Aunt Flossie was mistaken. She was pretty sure that Freddie had died. He'd been killed, just like Will Sapsworth, and had never come home to Dorothea.

It would be brilliant if he really had been wounded and sent home, a happy ending, but real life wasn't like that, was it? She couldn't allow herself to hope. Not without proof.

Freddie took more items out of the box and arranged them on a ledge. There was a tattered photograph album and a stiff cream envelope stuffed with more old pictures. There was a small brass cylinder with a mechanism of cogs at one end, which Esther guessed might be a lighter of some sort. There was a box containing two medals hung on coloured ribbons and, most exciting of all, a tiny glass bottle. Esther picked it up. It was no bigger than the palm of her hand and had a boat inside it just like the one she loved in her dad's collection. This boat had pretty green sails instead of red, matching the colours of the striped ribbon that had been tied in a bow around the bottle's neck. A shiver of delight bubbled up through her body. The stripes were purple, white and green, the suffragette colours.

Her heart now pumping hard in her chest, she opened the photograph album. Tucked into the front was a stack of modern coloured photographs – kids splashing in the sea, a boy on a red bike, a family waving from a window.

'That's my dad,' said Freddie. 'The boy on the bike.'

Esther nodded.

'My great-great-grandad is on the third page in. I've marked it.'

Esther slipped her finger behind a torn slip of paper sticking out near the spine and eased the album open. Fastened to black paper with little white tabs were four old photographs. On the left-hand page was a studio portrait of a teenage boy in uniform. Beside it was the same lad in civilian clothes standing on an orchard ladder. On the opposite page was a picture she'd seen before, the Black Lamb treasure hunt team. The last picture made Esther hold her breath. It was creased and crumpled, and the corners had been worn almost to curves. This was a photograph that had been handled, kept in a pocket perhaps, and brought out again and again to be viewed, caressed and treasured. It was of a girl with dark hair wearing a white dress. She looked about seventeen or eighteen, but if she'd had her hair tied in plaits and her cheeks were a little more puffed out, she could easily be the girl who wore the 'VOTES FOR WOMEN' sash, or the smiling treasure hunter.

. . . your picture, which lies in my breast pocket pressed against my heart.

Esther looked up at Freddie. 'Can I . . . um, can I take it out? I want to check something.'

Freddie nodded.

She put her fingernail under the edge of the picture and

prised it gently from the white tabs. The photo popped out into her hand and she turned it over. Written in blue biro were the words '*Mother 1915*', but beneath this, in pencil, were four faint looped lines.

Within a house that is not a house,
Search for all that is yours,
And a name that marks the end.
Hiding an impossible feat, tied with a bow.

Esther grinned.

'What does it mean?' Molly asked.

'It's a treasure hunt clue. She sent it to him in France.'

'Who?' said Molly.

'Dorothea. The girl.'

'Let's have a look,' said Gulliver. 'I'm good at treasure hunt clues.'

Esther handed it to him.

He read and thought and screwed up his face in concentration, then said, 'Nope. No idea,' and thrust it back at her.

Esther's grin grew broader. She'd got it almost instantly. She had never been good at working out clues, but she was in possession of a lot more knowledge than the others. She knew the person who'd written it.

'You know what it means, don't you?' said Molly.

'Uh-huh.' She leaned over, picked up the tiny pretty bottle and cradled it in her hand. 'It looks impossible to get a boat with mast and sails through the neck, but it's not. An impossible feat tied with a bow.'

'Cool!' said Freddie. 'The bottle is the treasure, then?'

'Which means someone found it.' Gulliver groaned, disappointed. 'I thought we were going to find a load of banknotes stashed away somewhere in a cave.'

'No, not in a cave. But I know where she did hide it,' said Esther, leaping to her feet and out of the boat. 'Come on. I'll show you.'

'Wait!' called Molly. 'Wait for us.'

The others followed her across the pebbles and up the concrete slipway to Dad's boathouse door.

'The boathouse!' cried Gull triumphantly. 'That's a house that's not a house. You see. I told you I was good at clues.' He walked up the ramp with his arms raised, making a hissing noise in the back of his throat like a roaring crowd. He turned left and right accepting imaginary applause.

'Dorothea's family owned this boathouse too,' said Esther. She leaned over and lifted a heavy rock near the top of the ramp and picked up the silver key hidden beneath. She slipped it into the brass padlock and it clicked open. All four of them pulled the doors open. Esther went straight over to the old photographs attached to the wall and found the carved brick she'd spotted a few days ago. The others were behind her.

'All that is yours is her heart,' she explained. She traced the edge of the heart shape. 'Her heart belonged to him.'

'Aww,' moaned Molly. 'How sweet.'

'Erh.' Gull rolled his eyes.

'A name that marks the end is dot, short for Dorothea,' Esther continued. She pointed to the circle beside the heart. It wasn't a circle, it was a dot. 'You see?'

'Behind the brick?' asked Freddie.

'I think so. It must be.' She dug her fingertips into the mortar and clawed at the edges, and slowly the brick began to shift. It scraped forward, brick and mortar rasping against each other, and finally dropped out on to the bench below, spilling a trickle of red dust. There was an alcove behind, just big enough to conceal the tiny bottle with the boat inside.

They all stared at the hole, then Esther put her hand into the gap. She held her breath and began to feel around, her fingertips and knuckles gently grazing the rough sides of the alcove. Then she touched something. It was dry and smooth. A cold thrill ran through her body as she pinched a fold of paper and pulled it out.

Treasure found.
Lighthouse path, Sunday, after church.
F. JWB

They followed Esther back outside. She was feeling light headed. She couldn't quite take it all in. She'd finally found Dotty and Freddie. The dark-haired girl in the photograph she was holding really had slept in her room at Pebbleton House, had loved Freddie, who had

written the letters she had found behind the fireplace. So why was she still unhappy?

She smoothed the fold of paper in one hand and caressed the bottle in the other. It wasn't enough. There was a piece of the puzzle missing. In a way it was the most important piece, the mystery that had sent her on her quest in the first place. Why didn't Dorothea send that letter? What had really happened to Freddie?

'What's wrong?' Molly asked.

'How can you be sure he wasn't killed?' Esther's voice wobbled. She was close to tears again.

'Duh!' Gulliver punched her on the shoulder. 'Haven't you been listening? He's Freddie's great-great-grandad. How could he be a grandfather if he died in the war, dummy? That's basic biology.'

'He might have been sent back,' Esther sobbed. 'It was only 1916. There were two more years left. He could have got better and been sent back. They were always sent back.'

'Oh.' Gulliver put the sunglasses back on.

Esther was dismayed. She still didn't have a definitive answer. How could she believe there was a happy ending to Dot and Freddie's story after reading the letters and knowing how much danger Freddie had faced? Two years was plenty of time to come home, marry Dot, make a baby, recover from his injuries and be pronounced fit enough to return to the front. She sat down on the concrete and put her head in her hands.

'You know,' said Gull, sitting down beside her. 'There's a really obvious way to find out.' He smirked. 'It's so obvious, Es, it's been staring you in the face.'

'What?' Esther asked, frowning.

'The war memorial, of course.'

Esther counted the names again. Thirty-nine. Thirty-nine men and boys from Pebbleton village had lost their lives in the Great War. Whole families had been wiped out, fathers, uncles, brothers, many Max's age and some not much older than Gulliver.

IN MEMORY OF
THE MEN OF PEBBLETON
WHO LOST THEIR LIVES
IN THE GREAT WAR
1914 - 1918

Charles Abbott 19
Cedric Adams 20
John Bailey 29
Edgar Bailey 26
Ralph Bishop 21
Henry Boyle 32
Ernest Clarke 18
Francis Clarke 20
Arthur Corfield 26
George Corfield 24
Harold Crocombe 22
Samuel Cooper 20
Joseph Cooper 18
George Duncan 36
Edwin Evans 25
James Evans 26
Ralph Fairlie 27
John Fraser 18
William Fraser 16

Alfred Gutteridge 35
John Gutteridge 17
Stanley Gutteridge 20
John Harding 27
William Harding 29
Cecil Hayward 20
Albert Higson 28
Frank Higson 26
Harry Jones 16
John Linford 19
William Padsfield 23
Frank Potter 19
Henry Sapsworth 46
John Sapsworth 21
William Sapsworth 19
Edmund Swain 15
James Swain 18
George Tricket 20
Edgar Webb 19
Timothy Webb 21

Frederick Blezzard's name was not among them. Freddie had survived. His family had been spared. Dorothea had been spared. Frederick had been injured and sent home, just as Aunt Flossie had said. But what had he come home to? A village empty of men, his childhood friends dead and buried in France. And across the country, every town, every small village like Pebbleton had a similar memorial, had suffered the same loss. A whole generation. Gone.

Esther sat on the war memorial steps. She wiped her cheeks and sniffed her tears away. Then she felt a hand slip into hers. This touch didn't cause her to crumble like the chalk cliff or to shatter into tiny pieces and blow away. This touch filled her heart and soothed her aching brain. This touch made her bones shiver and sent her stomach beetle spinning in happy circles. Without moving her head, she stole a look through trembling hair.

She knew it would be him.

Freddie.

'You OK?' he whispered.

She turned to him and smiled. She nodded and squeezed his hand.

'Yes, thanks. Much better now.'

The next few days were chaotic. Esther hardly had time to think. The film people left, Byron went back to London, to his girlfriend, and Molly got over it. Esther's bedroom was redecorated. It was painted bright blue, a delicious hue the exact colour of a cloudless midsummer sky. She'd almost requested purple again, but then decided against it. Purple was probably not a good idea. The fireplace was refixed firmly to the wall and no longer gaped or wobbled.

Dear Max,
Such a lot has happened since the storm and finding Freddie and going a bit loopy. Things have been better since the memorial. I don't mean it's great or back to the way it was – I don't suppose that will ever happen – it's just better, easier. There are no more secrets, no more lies, no more telling each other that we're fine when we're not. We are eating more meals together too, and talking more, sharing the pain of your absence. I think you're our war wound, Max, our missing limb. We'll need time to heal.

And now it's Mum's turn to go crazy. And I mean more crazy than usual! She's hardly slept this week. She's so excited about the Pebbleton Guest House Grand Reopening tomorrow. Typical Mum. She's got this whole media event planned, loads of local celebs, and she even got the film people to come back. The house does look amazing, especially the newly painted conservatory. We're fully booked until Christmas.

Dad applied for a job at the boatyard in Stone Harbour. I guess we always knew he liked building models, but did you have any idea he had sketchbooks full of fancy yacht designs? Me neither.

Oh! You won't believe this. Gull has a girlfriend! Yep, the freak actually found a girl who doesn't mind his Call of Duty addiction or hygiene phobia. I fear for her sanity!

I miss Freddie since he went home to his mum, but he calls and texts me every day and he'll be down for the half-term break. Yay!

Did I tell you that the movie is being dedicated to Frederick and Dorothea? Well, they found out about the letters – Mum told them, I think – and they were really interested and said they might make a little documentary about them. You know, like a 'behind the scenes' film for the DVD type of thing. They said we should donate them to a museum – with the ship in the bottle and the photographs and medals and stuff – so I thought I'd give them to the Pebbleton Museum. I don't think Freddie and Dotty would mind that too much.

We decided not to open her last letter. What she wrote was personal and private, only meant for Freddie, so we thought the envelope should remain sealed. For ever.

You were an amazing brother, Max. The best. And you taught me such a lot. Your dying taught me a lot too. It's been hard and I still miss you. I'll always miss you, always remember you. But I'm not going to write again.

Goodbye, Max.

Love and all that cheesy stuff,

Your sister,

Egg

x

John Keats
1795 – 1821

When I Have Fears

When I have fears that I may cease to be
  Before my pen has glean'd my teeming brain,
Before high-piled books, in charactery,
  Hold like rich garners the full ripen'd grain;
When I behold, upon the night's starr'd face,
  Huge cloudy symbols of a high romance,
And think that I may never live to trace
  Their shadows, with the magic hand of chance;
And when I feel, fair creature of an hour,
  That I shall never look upon thee more,
Never have relish in the faery power
  Of unreflecting love;–then on the shore
Of the wide world I stand alone, and think
Till Love and Fame to nothingness do sink.

Ode to a Nightingale

My heart aches, and a drowsy numbness pains
    My sense, as though of hemlock I had drunk,
Or emptied some dull opiate to the drains
    One minute past, and Lethe-wards had sunk:
'Tis not through envy of thy happy lot,
    But being too happy in thine happiness, –
        That thou, light-winged Dryad of the trees,
          In some melodious plot
    Of beechen green and shadows numberless,
      Singest of summer in full-throated ease.

O, for a draught of vintage! that hath been
    Cool'd a long age in the deep-delved earth,
Tasting of Flora and the country green,
    Dance, and Provençal song, and sunburnt mirth!
O for a beaker full of the warm South,
    Full of the true, the blushful Hippocrene,
        With beaded bubbles winking at the brim,
          And purple-stained mouth;
    That I might drink, and leave the world unseen,
      And with thee fade away into the forest dim:

Fade far away, dissolve, and quite forget
    What thou among the leaves hast never known,
The weariness, the fever, and the fret
    Here, where men sit and hear each other groan;
Where palsy shakes a few, sad, last gray hairs,
    Where youth grows pale, and spectre-thin, and dies;
        Where but to think is to be full of sorrow
            And leaden-eyed despairs,
    Where Beauty cannot keep her lustrous eyes,
        Or new Love pine at them beyond to-morrow.

Away! away! for I will fly to thee,
    Not charioted by Bacchus and his pards,
But on the viewless wings of Poesy,
    Though the dull brain perplexes and retards:
Already with thee! tender is the night,
    And haply the Queen-Moon is on her throne,
        Cluster'd around by all her starry Fays;
            But here there is no light,
    Save what from heaven is with the breezes blown
        Through verdurous glooms and winding mossy
            ways.

I cannot see what flowers are at my feet,
    Nor what soft incense hangs upon the boughs,
But, in embalmed darkness, guess each sweet
    Wherewith the seasonable month endows
The grass, the thicket, and the fruit-tree wild;
    White hawthorn, and the pastoral eglantine;
        Fast fading violets cover'd up in leaves;
            And mid-May's eldest child,
    The coming musk-rose, full of dewy wine,
        The murmurous haunt of flies on summer eves.

Darkling I listen; and, for many a time
    I have been half in love with easeful Death,
Call'd him soft names in many a mused rhyme,
    To take into the air my quiet breath;
Now more than ever seems it rich to die,
    To cease upon the midnight with no pain,
        While thou art pouring forth thy soul abroad
            In such an ecstasy!
    Still wouldst thou sing, and I have ears in vain –
        To thy high requiem become a sod.

Thou wast not born for death, immortal Bird!
　　No hungry generations tread thee down;
The voice I hear this passing night was heard
　　In ancient days by emperor and clown:
Perhaps the self-same song that found a path
　　Through the sad heart of Ruth, when, sick for home,
　　　She stood in tears amid the alien corn;
　　　　The same that oft-times hath
　　Charm'd magic casements, opening on the foam
　　Of perilous seas, in faery lands forlorn.

Forlorn! the very word is like a bell
　　To toll me back from thee to my sole self!
Adieu! the fancy cannot cheat so well
　　As she is fam'd to do, deceiving elf.
Adieu! adieu! thy plaintive anthem fades
　　Past the near meadows, over the still stream,
　　　Up the hill-side; and now 'tis buried deep
　　　　In the next valley-glades:
　　Was it a vision, or a waking dream?
　　Fled is that music: – Do I wake or sleep?

Wilfred Owen
1893 – 1918

ANTHEM FOR DOOMED YOUTH

What passing-bells for these who die as cattle?
   Only the monstrous anger of the guns.
Only the stuttering rifles' rapid rattle
   Can patter out their hasty orisons.
No mockeries now for them; no prayers nor bells;
   Nor any voice of mourning save the choirs, –
The shrill, demented choirs of wailing shells;
   And bugles calling for them from sad shires.

What candles may be held to speed them all?
   Not in the hands of boys but in their eyes
Shall shine the holy glimmers of goodbyes.
   The pallor of girls' brows shall be their pall;
Their flowers the tenderness of patient minds,
   And each slow dusk a drawing-down of blinds.

FUTILITY

Move him into the sun –
Gently its touch awoke him once,
At home, whispering of fields half-sown.
Always it woke him, even in France,
Until this morning and this snow.
If anything might rouse him now
The kind old sun will know.

Think how it wakes the seeds –
Woke once the clays of a cold star.
Are limbs, so dear achieved, are sides
Full-nerved, still warm, too hard to stir?
Was it for this the clay grew tall?
– O what made fatuous sunbeams toil
To break earth's sleep at all?

STRANGE MEETING

It seemed that out of the battle I escaped
Down some profound dull tunnel, long since scooped
Through granites which Titanic wars had groined.
Yet also there encumbered sleepers groaned,
Too fast in thought or death to be bestirred.
Then, as I probed them, one sprang up, and stared
With piteous recognition in fixed eyes,
Lifting distressful hands, as if to bless.
And by his smile, I knew that sullen hall,
By his dead smile, I knew we stood in Hell.
With a thousand fears that vision's face was grained;
Yet no blood reached there from the upper ground,
And no guns thumped, or down the flues made moan.
'Strange friend,' I said, 'here is no cause to mourn.'
'None,' said the other, 'Save the undone years,
The hopelessness. Whatever hope is yours,
Was my life also; I went hunting wild
After the wildest beauty in the world,
Which lies not calm in eyes, or braided hair,
But mocks the steady running of the hour,
And if it grieves, grieves richlier than here.
For by my glee might many men have laughed,
And of my weeping something has been left,
Which must die now. I mean the truth untold,
The pity of war, the pity war distilled.
Now men will go content with what we spoiled,
Or, discontent, boil bloody, and be spilled.

They will be swift with swiftness of the tigress.
None will break ranks, though nations trek from progress.
Courage was mine, and I had mystery,
Wisdom was mine, and I had mastery:
To miss the march of this retreating world
Into vain citadels that are not walled.
Then, when much blood had clogged their chariot-wheels
I would go up and wash them from sweet wells,
Even with truths that lie too deep for taint.
I would have poured my spirit without stint
But not through wounds; not on the cess of war.
Foreheads of men have bled where no wounds were.
I am the enemy you killed, my friend.
I knew you in this dark: for so you frowned
Yesterday through me as you jabbed and killed.
I parried; but my hands were loath and cold.
Let us sleep now . . .'

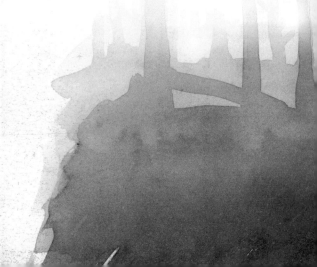

Acknowledgements

Thank you to everyone who generously shared with me their own poignant family stories from 100 years ago. Particular thanks to Sally Todd for your marvellous WW1 book lists and for being a super-librarian. And words can not describe my gratitude to Hannah, Penny, Sam and my mum for keeping me sane... ish.